WILDLY WEDDED WIFE

WIFE

᭡BOOK 2᭡

BLENDED

WILDLY WEDDED WIFE

Copyright ©2014 Erica Chilson

www.ericachilson.com/wicked-reads

Printed in the United States of America
First Printing, 2017
ISBN-13: 978-0-9979899-2-2
ISBN-10: 0-9979899-2-0

A NOTE FROM THE WICKED WRITER:

As my writing style has evolved, it's been very difficult for me to write something short & sweet. Even reading a novella, short story, or serial storyline is difficult for me. I'm always left wanting more. More everything: more story, more character development, more of the what, where, how, why, when, and who. The meaty stuff that makes a story compelling. As a reader who always demands more, it causes the writer in me to demand more out of myself. Hence the reason why both Good Girl & Widow are nearly pushing 700 pages, and Lord help us when I get to my M&M rewrites of the Queen Omnibus & Faithless. QO is already well over 1,200 pages…

Not everyone reads as I do, craves more. Some love short & sweet– a quick escape from the everyday normalcy of life.

As I was writing Widow, the need to voice the side characters became apparent. I wanted the main series to stick to the members of the blended family, but their friends and coworkers were chatting with me, demanding a voice. This gave me the opportunity for several things: show I can write a novella, not only to myself but to my readers who didn't think I had it in me, as well as explain why an author writes as he/she does.

THE WHY OF IT:

I've seen many a review on novellas dealing with long-standing series, with readers complaining about how if properly developed, expanded, lengthened, the story would have been better. They always ask **WHY**. Why did the author choose to short-change this character and not the others? Well, I will tell you why. I'm answering for myself, but I feel I will hit the answer with the majority of the authors in question.

The entirety of the Blended series was written in my head before I started writing Widow. All the books in the series, so any other books would just wreck it: my outlines, the outcomes, the timelines, the release dates. That is where you get novellas and short stories– these are the stories the author wishes to tell, but will ultimately ruin the flow of the series if incorporated in the series as a full-length novel. They are also the characters that have a need to only show a singular event, without going into greater detail. (Our characters, the muse, and the series itself is what forces authors to write. We are not in the driver's seat at any given time) Also, with Blended, I wanted to keep the main series strictly to the members of the Blended family. There you have it.

That's why I created the novellas. Why many authors of long-standing series create their novellas. Why readers ask why this character and not another...

DID THE WICKED WRITER SUCCEED?

As there are rules for every aspect of writing, there are for novellas as well. (Not a serial. *shudders*). The story must have a beginning, middle, and an ending, all wrapped up in a short package with a tidy bow. That means you must have fast-pacing, absolutely no filler, hardly any descriptions, and a rapid flow of scenes evolving over a short period of time, which are cohesive yet show the story in which you wish to tell. In order to fit this criteria, most of the time, character development, sexual tension, and the story itself are lost. I call short stories and novellas **instant gratification**. The romance always borders on insta-love, the sex is without buildup, and the major conflict is light. There is truly nothing an author can do about this, given so few pages he/she must use to evolve the story. Proof I hate having guidelines I must follow.

For my first foray into the world of novellas, I tried my damnedest to maintain my love of character development. In order to eliminate the insta-love, I had to write a quick backstory & **tell** the readers, not **show** them, that the characters were **in** love. Hopefully I succeeded in proving there was sustainability in the future with the couple by their actions. As for the conflict, I saw this as a fabulous way to show another side of our sometimes-villain, sometimes-sweetheart, all-the-time Mr. Kline. None of the other characters would be in a position to show Auggie in this light, so I went for it, and in doing so, I set up the events in Wayward.

So... as you read Wildly Wedded Wife, and say to yourself, "Erica, I wish you would have expanded on this or that," remember I had a certain criteria to fill, and to do anything else would have pushed me into novel territory. I was slowly encroaching as it was, and had to cut myself off. So when you decide you wanted more of the past, more brightly colored chalk on a sidewalk, more puppy time, remember... and then simply use your imagination to fill in the blanks. I built the foundation, the rest is up to you.

Bethany Oman: Another six months and my thesis will be finished, and then I can stop this suffocating charade. My dream is to become a therapist specializing in sexual dysfunction. What better way to write my thesis than in a Playroom filled with sexual deviants? Only problem, I had to become a deviant in order to gain entrance to the Playroom… and then I had to explain my motivations to Augustus Kline, who offered me protection for a very steep toll.

My other dream is standing before me, smirking with anticipation. My original, lifelong-dream, who could easily destroy any hope of my becoming a therapist if I'm not careful.

And Rory Essex makes me feel anything but careful.

Willing to do anything it takes to gain the woman he loves, Rory makes a deal with Beth, which forces him to bargain with the Devil Himself.

Accepting Augustus Kline's toll into the Playroom, Rory gains the key to making Bethany his Wildly Wedded Wife.

PRESENT

Bethany Oman

Stretching causes a loud groan to bubble up my throat. My God, I fucking hurt. I flex my muscles, trying to discern why they ache. I've been in two car accidents in my time, and they didn't hurt this badly. Those were fender-benders, and I feel as if I've been in a head-on collision with an eighteen-wheeler while in my sleep.

Wiggling around on the mattress, I try to find a comfortable spot. It's so dark in my room that I know I'm not due back at the salon for at least another few hours. Meaning, I should get up and put in a few hours on my thesis before I have to go in and stand on my feet for eight hours, washing hair and hating every second of it. I groan, dreading the endless small-talk with my patrons and the fallen arches of my soles.

I love people, but I love analyzing them more. What's difficult to swallow is the repetition of conversation: *the weather has been lovely/horrid/cold/hot/wet/dry. How is your daughter/son/brother/daughter/wife/husband? Yes, I'd love to hear about your medical ailments again.*

I was not cut out to cut hair for a living. I'm naturally chatty and completely weirded out by uncomfortable silence, so I've been dubbed a talker to fill the void while I style hair. I was born for one-on-one in a cozy office space, with all conversation centered on my patients' issues.

Stretching again, did I stay up too late writing on my thesis again? No, it's definitely more than a crick in the neck, and I'm not hugging my laptop like a pillow either.

"Ouch!" I yelp in pain when my thighs rub together. "Ow… ow… ow, that really freakin' hurts." Whimpering, I notice that the soreness is concentrated between my thighs. My puss feels beat up, bruised, ridden too hard, and rode again. I think back, memory foggy…

The one time Auggie screwed the hell out of me versus his usual kind routine, I wasn't this bad off. If the Beast couldn't harm me, what the hell did?

The further awake I become, the more noticeable the pain becomes. All the sore spots on my body are from being manhandled. Dimpled fingertip bruises, no doubt. Fiery pain shoots along my nerves when my nipples brush against the sheet covering me.

Room blanketed in darkness, I reach over to my side lamp. I need to check out my injuries before my imagination runs wild. My hand meets dead air. "What. The. Fuck?" I reach farther, still not finding my Hello Kitty lamp. Now that I'm awake, I realize the sheet covering me is not my Hello Kitty, fuzzy flannel sheet set, and the mattress beneath me is not twin-sized with springs jabbing into my ribcage.

Fear floods my veins as my mind rationalizes that I am NOT in my bedroom at home. My body has been ravaged, and I don't know how or by whom. As a woman on the cusp of a Master's in Psychology, working on her thesis, this scares the shit out of me.

Panting heavily into the dark room, my body tells me it's mid-morning but the room itself is as dark as a coffin. My brain floods my body with a mixture of chemicals that set off a chain reaction: shaking, skin beading with gooseflesh, and sweat coating my skin as terror takes its hold.

"Little Pup," comes from a deep, husky voice. The sound of sheets shifting, as his body moves around on the bed, is loud to my hypersensitive ears.

The terror intensifies as I realize I am NOT the only occupant in this room, in this *bed*. Muscles bunching for flight, I take a deep breath, prepared to run even though I can't see.

"Bethany?" The tight voice is frustrated with me. "What is up with you, girl?"

A meaty palm reaches out to connect with my hand, squeezing as if to reassure me. I squeak, panicked. That huge hand put a beating on me. This man in bed with me has used and abused my body until it hurts so badly I can barely move. My heart starts to beat so rapidly I fear I'm going to have an attack–heart or panic, I don't know which.

Hand retracting, "Beth, goddamn it," he snarls as if disappointed in my rejecting his touch. Flesh slides on the sheets as he rolls to the edge of the bed. With him moving farther away from me, I take a deep breath and try to come up with an escape plan.

With an audible click, light floods the room, burning my eyes and causing me to blink repeatedly until my vision returns. Haloed in the light, he is a large fuzzy visage I can't quite make out.

"Are you blind?" he asks wryly as I blink up at him. Amusement is thick in his raspy voice. "Hung over, perhaps?" He chuckles to himself like he finds my terror entertaining, "Amnesiac?" I diagnose him as a sociopath right on the spot. Sounding way too pleased with himself, with a level of arrogance that pushes him into narcissism. Settling back against his pillow, he murmurs with utter satisfaction, "Give it a minute. It will all come flooding back in."

Between one blink and the next, he proves himself not arrogant but correct. "Motherfuck," I snarl, flailing around the bed in a fit of anger, not even giving a shit that it makes the pain between my thighs worse. "You tricked me, asshole!"

Blue eyes sparkling with mischief and pure pleasure, sinful lips displaying a Cheshire cat smile, and one single dimple in his cheek, Rory crashes my world down around me. "Did you sleep well, Mrs. Essex?"

CHAPTER ONE

36 hours earlier…

It's odd, coming to Rush without the Playroom being in the back anymore. We've been in a transitional phase as we await Willow's go-ahead to open the Spook House's attic as the new Playroom. The Playroom at Rush has been shut down for weeks as we wait, but that doesn't negate my obligation to Auggie. I understand Auggie and Robin's need to relocate it, but I hate having to come to Rush first to loosen up. One of these days, I'll get pulled over for a DUI on the drive from Rush to the Spook House. I just can't… I just can't be around Augustus Kline without some liquid courage first.

Worse than a DUI is Rush's bouncer. I might have to take up drinking in my car outside of the Spook House just to avoid the man. But rumor has it, Chief Mason is looking to buy that huge pink house across the street. I think I'd rather take my chances on the road versus the Chief arresting me for public intoxication outside of his front door.

Another six months and my thesis will be finished, and then I can stop this suffocating charade. My dream is to become a therapist, specializing in sexual dysfunction. What better way to write my thesis than in a Playroom filled with sexual deviants? Only problem, I had to become a deviant in order to gain entrance to the Playroom… and then I had to explain my motivations to Augustus Kline, who offered me protection for a very steep toll.

My other dream is standing before me, smirking with anticipation. My original, lifelong-dream, who could easily destroy any hope of my becoming a therapist if I'm not careful.

And Rory Essex makes me feel anything but careful.

Barring my way inside the club is the bouncer in question, the bane of my existence, the man who makes my pulse speed in anticipation. I should find Rory intimidating, not drool-worthy.

The man has made my knees wobbly weak and my panties sopping wet since I figured out what that sensation meant back when I was an infatuated twelve-year-old girl.

Always has.

Always will.

At a good foot taller than me, and at least two hundred and fifty pounds, Rory is a mammoth man. Instead of his hulking size frightening me, it makes me feel safe… which is the real reason I'm so very much afraid of my childhood neighbor. If I give in to what we both want, my future is in jeopardy.

Genuinely happy to see me, eager even, smiling, "Little Pup," Rory teases, causing my face to twist up into a grimace.

Like a troll guarding a bridge, awaiting their toll, Rory leans against the door, refusing to let me pass until he gets to speak his piece. His thickly muscled arms are crossed over his well-defined chest as a silent threat. I swallow a whimper, hating this mating dance.

Loving this mating dance.

Getting off on it just as much as Rory does.

Thankfully, it's a slow night at Rush, or else I'd have a line of angry customers behind me. But Thursdays are usually very slow. The customers' paychecks dried up by Sunday night, leaving them to work for the '*man*' for the rest of the week to pay for another round of weekend fun. It's a vicious cycle I am glad I'm not a part of.

My annoyance isn't feigned. "Rory, don't call me that," I beg for the billionth time. "You know I hate it."

I hate having to playact a puppy– **LOATHE** it. It makes it worse because Rory has heard stories about my exploits, and he teases me relentlessly because of it. I never wanted my lifelong friend to know how I've reduced myself for the sake of advancement. If you look at it from a certain, unfavorable angle, I've whored myself out in my quest to earn that coveted degree. I've become the type of person I will counsel in the future.

Lovely.

I'll be analyzing the parallels for the rest of my career.

Eyes heavily lidded as he gazes down at me, "Go out with me tomorrow," Rory presses, just like he does every single time I see him. "We can go to the city for a nice meal before I have to be back at Rush. Or we could just take a walk if it's going to be nice out." He sounds so hopeful that it kills me. Voice filled with equal parts frustration and ache, "Even if we just sit in your car and chat in the parking lot. Something, Bethany– *please*."

Rory reaches out to tuck a strand of my hair behind my ear, and it takes everything in me not to press into his touch. We both sigh– both of us annoyed with my reluctance.

I've been in love with Rory Essex since the day I rushed out my front door to find him playing with chalk on the sidewalk in front of our houses. I was four and he was seven. Instant friends, Rory reached up, handing me a big, pink stick of chalk. I sat down beside him and started drawing hearts next to his stick-figure family. We spent the rest of Rory's summer vacation decorating the entire block of sidewalks, creating the story of our lives... until it was washed off during a strong downpour. Heartbroken, Rory mended me by starting the process all over again the next morning. I awoke to a rainbow of color when I looked out my bedroom window.

Too young, I realized the heartbreak of washed-away dreams paled in comparison to being left behind– a path in life I've been on since September of my fourth year. I was probably the first kid in all of history who begged to go to school early. Like a puppy awaiting its best friend, it was a long year of waiting at the front window at three o'clock every afternoon for Rory to get off of the school bus. More often than not, he never acknowledged my silly, little girl existence. After all, Rory was a big kid with big kid friends.

I cried, great wracking sobs, when I finally got to kindergarten, only to learn we weren't all dumped into the same classroom. Rory was over in the third grade, while I was sequestered with the littlest kids. Eager for first grade, so we could finally share a playground together at recess, again I was devastated. Chasing broken dreams, I learned fourth graders were in another building, with another playground.

I spent the rest of my school career chasing Rory Essex, never quite catching up to him. He graduated when I was still a girl. After I graduated high school, Essie and I went to cosmology school. As soon as I was licensed, I continued my education. I've been in school ever since, while working at the salon to pay for more tuition. No longer living next door to my parents and me, I finally saw Rory again when I showed up at Rush for my thesis quest at the Playroom.

Now it's Rory's turn to chase me, because he's where he will always be, but I've yet to arrive at my final destination.

Six more months.

My usual answer to Rory's '*go out with me*' request rolls right off my tongue, "I can't," and it frustrates Rory to no end, but not nearly as much as it frustrates me.

Disappointment is evident in his rejection-filled voice. "Why not?" is how Rory always replies.

Going by the script, "I'm busy."

Gritting out between clenched teeth, "So busy you're hanging out at Rush on a slow night." Not going by the script, "Don't you like me?" Looking thoroughly depressed, Rory cracks my heart open, causing a lump to form in my throat.

My eyes close on their own, refusing to look up to the slab of male perfection before me. The twenty-five-year-old guy is tall, muscular, and pretty. Pretty like a girl, with big watery blue eyes and dimples. So pretty, Rory shaves his honey-brown hair close to his scalp to look manlier. Not that he needs any help in that department. He looks like he cracks spines for shits 'n giggles, and then fucks the first girl who his eyes fall upon. From the sexual potency of Rory's stormy gaze, the panties of the girl he picks just fall off, and the flames from her puss are doused from the well of arousal between her thighs.

I would know– I've been volunteering for that position since I was twelve, and Rory hadn't even matured into a man yet. I haven't had dry panties since I hit puberty, and I'm pretty sure my panties ignited when I first showed up to Rush to find Rory barring the door. I feel bare-naked without 'em.

"We've been through this shit, Rory," I groan out. "Doing the same thing over and over and expecting a different result is a sign of insanity. You want a girlfriend, and I can't have a boyfriend yet. Ask me again when I've got my degree, and the answer will be a '*hell, yes!*' It's only six months. You can wait that long."

Taking my '*hell, yes*' as an invitation to get into my personal space, Rory leans down into me. The heat radiating off of the large man warms me to my core. Our faces inches apart, Rory's breath flutters against my lips as he speaks. "I would never take that away from you," he fiercely vows. "I don't see why you can't date me and go to school at the same time. You're confusing me."

I know I'm confusing Rory, and he is highly intelligent. He's not just Rush's bouncer– he's the manager. He's not some deadbeat townie who peaked in high school. Rory Essex is my future, but only after I finish what I've started.

So frustrated I'm suffocating, I'm unable to answer Rory truthfully, as usual. I'm not avoiding Rory because I think he would force me to quit school and become his housewife. But it is school that keeps me away– my thesis is contingent on the Playroom.

Auggie gave me to Opal with the puppy routine to keep the members from following me around. He also has sex with me in public every once in awhile to keep the relentless men off my ass. The night a guy shoved his fingers up my crotch, wedded the first night I went to Auggie with the truth, and I paid Auggie's steep toll willingly and gladly.

My entrance toll into the Playroom– Auggie went down on me. My toll for protection– sex twice a month for the duration of my stay. Morally, I can't fuck Auggie if I have a boyfriend. But if I don't, I'm free meat in the Playroom.

I'm in a lose-lose situation, no matter how badly I may want Rory.

My eyes are closed as I'm lost in thought. My mind spins around my impossible situation, wishing I could find a feasible solution. I must look like an idiot, standing at the entrance to Rush with Rory leaning over me. There are people waiting to get into the club, but they can't until Rory opens the door, and he's not going to move until I relent and go on a date with him. This is our standard modus operandi.

Taking it as a good sign when I keep my eyes closed and don't push him out of my orbit, Rory initiates. A heavy breath sighs out of me when Rory softly brushes his lips across mine. I lean into our very first intimate touch as adults, mystified over the difference eight years can make.

My first kiss was Rory. Puberty, raging hormones, Essie's encouraging lunacy, all had me doing something unbelievably stupid. I had just turned thirteen, and Rory was about to turn seventeen. I saw Rory sitting on the top step of his front porch, playing around on his cellphone. The spur-of-the-moment idea took root, and like an idiot, I went with it. In a fumbling attempt, I caught him unaware. I managed to get my lips to land on Rory's for a split-second before he shoved my ass to the ground. Ass bruised, palms scuffed, I stared up at Rory from the sidewalk with tears in my eyes. Devastated and ashamed, I knew I'd fucked up our friendship, and there was no going back.

Eyes glowing with a furious light, "You can't just go around kissing people, Bethany," Rory admonished me. "What if they don't wanna kiss ya back?"

Rejection flowing in my veins, with no answer for Rory's question, I took off running to lick my wounds in private.

Afterward, worried I'd attack him, Rory wouldn't get within ten feet of me. Every time I walked outside, he'd go back inside. Every time he came out of his house to find me in the front lawn, he'd run to his car, starting it before I could even blink, driving away from me as usual. He made me feel like I was a stalker– a predator.

Shame made me stop chasing Rory.

A year later, Rory graduated, grew up, started working for Isis, and moved across town to live above Rush. I'd spy Rory visiting his parents from time to time, but he'd only give me a wave of acknowledgement before disappearing into the depths of his parents' house.

Eight years later, with a handful of sightings and a dozen '*go out with me*' requests, now Rory is the one chasing after me. I could blame my thesis quest. But as an aspiring therapist, I recognize how I secretly love turning the tables on Rory.

It's Rory Essex's turn to beg.

My hands fly out, palms landing squarely into the center of Rory's broad chest. I shove with all my might, forcing Rory to fall. He doesn't fall down three steps to land on his butt on the sidewalk like I did. He doesn't bloody his palms and bruise his backside. No, Rory simply slumps against Rush's entrance door, just as shocked and confused as I was eight years ago– ego smashed by rejection, a sensation I know all too well.

The waiting line behind me gasps, amazed that I just assaulted Rush's ornery manager. "You can't just go around kissing people, Rory," I mock. "What if they don't wanna kiss ya back?"

Blue eyes held wide, stunned, it takes a few seconds for my words to fully sink in, and then Rory releases a laugh that is equal parts irony and amusement. Righting himself, he opens the door to the club. "Touché, Little Pup," Rory roughly whispers to me, brushing his lips against my hair, as I walk by to enter Rush.

CHAPTER TWO

Leaning on Rush's bar, I'd only planned on having a few drinks to loosen myself up before I made my way over to the Spook House. I wanted to get lubricated (inebriated) for my bi-weekly sex with Auggie. Not that I don't enjoy my time with the sexy beast of a man– it's just creepy.

Augustus Kline has a strange set of morals he lives by, and it's those morals that creep me out as much as fascinate me. I could build my career on the mysteries of Auggie's wounded psyche.

In my thesis quest, I had my ear trained on any nefarious activities in the area. With a gossip queen for a best friend, Essie always has the best information. When drunk, Essie chatters about anything and everything, and the girl kept telling me about Robin Prynne's sexual deviancy. I was a hairsbreadth away from contacting Rob when I heard a rumor about the mysterious Playroom. Fairport's rumor mill pointed out Augustus Kline as the man to see. Easy enough to locate, I went to see Auggie.

Eager and determined, I'd cornered Auggie at Rush, just as he was coming out of the stairwell leading up to Isis's loft…

Startling Auggie, "I want to join the Playroom," was the first thing out of my mouth.

Backing up like he was scared of me, all the while shaking his head no. Auggie even said no out loud while pulling a complementary gesture of denial. Voice thick, "No. Trust me. You don't want to join the Playroom."

"Why not?" Angry and confused, I needed the Playroom or I was sunk. What else could a Fairport girl use for her thesis on sexual deviancy? It was perfect, and it was right in my own backyard.

Serious, Auggie stared me down with his piercing green eyes, baring me raw as if he could see straight into my soul.

"*Bethany, you're going to be a good man's wife someday. I can't in good conscience treat you like a whore.*"

"*I'm not a whore,*" I agreed emphatically. "*I can have sex, though. I'm in no way a virgin. If you make it through college with your innocence intact, then you were doing it wrong,*" I teased in a sultry voice, earning myself a wide-toothed grin and a furry russet eyebrow raise.

Clearing his throat, like what I said disturbed him in a sexual way, "*Fair enough.*" Auggie gazed at his boots, fingers roughly combing through his wild red hair. Clearing his throat again, "*Everyone pays a toll to enter the Playroom, sweet cheeks,*" Auggie warned, acting like he hoped to scare me off. "*Since you're not a whore, I can't make you blow me or fuck me like one. So...*" heavy pause where he considers. "*If you let me go down on you, you can join the Playroom.*"

"*Serious?*" I squeak, shocked at the aroused excitement that flared through my nether region. "*Let me get this straight... the toll is me getting off, not you?*" Auggie nodded his head yes, looking faintly shocked himself that I was so accepting of his costly toll. "*Where do I sign up?*"

I eagerly paid my toll a few minutes later… leaning against Auggie's office door, his large palms spreading my thighs wide while his tongue lapped and his lips feasted at my lust-moistened flesh. It was the finest oral sex of my life, earning me three orgasms while Auggie used his palm to rub himself off over top of his jeans. I had a wicked headache the next day from my head falling back against the door in ecstasy, repeatedly thumping in time with my orgasms.

I've enjoyed Augustus Kline's oral pleasure several times a week for almost a year. I was by no means a virgin when I went to him. Auggie has been my lover– my first true lover –fumbling teenage boys do not count. All man, Auggie placed his ownership on me. Opal is a ruse to explain why Auggie isn't sharing my ass with every dick and pussy in the Playroom. My childlike puppy routine seems to act as a good deterrent, naked as I am.

Opal Fischer should be my very first patient. The woman wants to be in the Playroom yet she doesn't want to participate. Everyone has a reason they're in the Playroom, but I've yet to ferret out Opal's motivations. I'm Opal's excuse as much as she is mine. She sends me cute thank you presents every time we do our routine. I feel like a kept woman, but I do enjoy the impromptu gifts: lotions and perfumes, my favorite shows on

Blu-ray, and Amazon and iTunes gift cards. We became insta-friends, so we know each other's likes and dislikes. I'm a poor college student, so Opal hardly ever gets gifts back from me. I do give her a wash and trim at the salon every two weeks. I'll give Opal free therapy sessions once I get my license. Joking.

No, I'm not.

If I could base my practice around the Playroomers, I'd be in business for life.

"Beth, you still there, darling?" Kylie's sugary-sweet voice yanks me from my thoughts. Rush's curvy bartender points at my shot glass, silently asking me if I want another.

Overenthusiastically slapping another three bucks onto the bar, my palm stings a bit. "Yeah, hit me with another," I try to sound all badassed, but my words slur together.

Snorting, Kylie rolls her large hazel eyes at me. "Gee, girl. I don't know if I should. This peach schnapps is some powerful shit," teasing me with her usual shtick. Flashing me a smile as she pours me another round, Kylie's beauty mark is on full display.

Kylie's like a modern day Marilyn Monroe, all pleasing curves, naturally blonde hair, and a beauty mark above her full lips. If it wasn't for the fact that she is a larger girl, she'd have men all over her, which makes me think men are fucking stupid. Kylie is a classic beauty where today's standard seems to be edging toward smutty trash that reeks of desperation. Guys are just too lazy to pursue a real woman who doesn't just give herself away for free, I guess.

Realizing I can't change the world, I shake my head back and forth in mild disgust. Thirst winning out, I snicker at myself as I pour my sixth shot of the night into my mouth, almost choking on it.

"You don't usually drink so much, Beth," Fairport's town drunk saddles up next to me on a barstool. Kylie slaps an unopened bottle of Wild Turkey and a shot glass in front of Matt.

"Matt, you're here for the same reason I am," I say pointedly. "Thursdays are half-priced drinks. I'm too cheap to come any other night."

Thank God, half-priced night just so happens to coincide with my bi-weekly courtesan duties, or I'd have to beg, borrow, and steal to pay for my liquid courage. Every other Thursday night belongs to Augustus Kline, and sometimes Robin Prynne too. Compoundedly, after every time, it is harder to do it the next time.

"We had to market it as such, or there wouldn't be a soul in here." Kylie slumps against the bar, sighing. "Dead in here except for Friday and Saturday, and then it's so packed I want to take an icepick to my brain to deaden the sound of the blaring music and the screaming skanks."

"Why don't you just use the icepick and shank the screaming skanks," I offer, giggling. "I've drank way over my limit," I admit, and not for the first time. Slurring, "I'll take another, pretty please with a peach on top." Finding myself impossibly hilarious, I laugh for a good minute straight.

Kylie and Matt just shake their heads at me in unison, causing my eyes to do the wiggle-waggle.

Calculating my funds, "That only puts me a buck over my twenty dollar limit." I grin, all proud that I still have the ability to do basic addition and multiplication. 3 x 7 = 21. Go me!

Pouring me another, Kylie muses about my drinking habits. Bartenders are the therapists of the alcoholic world after all—we're kindred. "I don't know what you have to do on Thursday nights that makes you need to get hammered beforehand. But it would be a lot cheaper if you'd just ask Isis to sell you a bottle of schnapps, or drive to the next county to the liquor store."

Perking up, sounding so chipper my ears ring, "Isis will do that? At cost? Isn't that illegal? I could make a bottle last nearly a month."

"Who's gonna arrest Isis?" Kylie says to me like I'm fucking insane. "Five bucks over cost. Why do you think good ol' Matt is here? Isis makes him drink his purchases at the bar so it looks like we have some customers. There are three patrons drinking under-the-shelf booze in here tonight, not counting the non-drinking dance floor fornicators and their drunken spectators."

"True," Matt murmurs while he pours himself another shot of Wild Turkey, proving it's his bottle, not the bar's. "I buy a bottle every night, except for the weekend."

"Why not the weekend? Does Isis throw your drunk ass out?" I taunt the thirty-something guy, who would be okay looking if he wasn't a raging alcoholic. Plus, Fairport's finest arrest Matt once or twice a week when he gets belligerent and starts fights with whomever meant him no insult.

"Those skanks," he whispers to me like a juicy secret, whiskey breath burning my nostrils, "Steal my barstool. I'd love to icepick 'em, but that would be illegal."

"Far be it from you to do anything illegal," I slur, sounding serious. Matt nods his head in agreement.

"Oh, Lord," Kylie draws out. "You drunk fucks are imbeciles." In a voice leaking industrial strength sarcasm, "Excuse me while I serve the girl who thought a sports bra and boy shorts were appropriate attire for our friendly neighborhood establishment."

Leaning into me as we sit side-by-side on our barstools, "Why do you get drunk?" Matt asks me, as if the answer is a secret.

"Just my day of the week to unwind," I lie flawlessly, because the answer is, in fact, a secret I will never voice aloud.

The truth– I need to be borderline drunk to get through the Playroom experience, but more so when it's my bi-weekly sex session. Who in their right mind could playact a puppy without being inebriated? Plus, Auggie won't *fuck* me because I'm not a whore– well, once I was fucked, and it was incredible, painful, and unforgettable. I've begged for a repeat, but I always get shut down.

Bi-weekly, I'm Auggie's *girlfriend* experience. Auggie makes *love* to me, all the while thinking of Isis, calling me Isis, murmuring his adoration for Isis in my ear while thrusting into me. Sometimes Auggie cries afterward.

There is a room at the Spook House that is for my courtesan duties. No one is allowed in there but me. Every other Thursday night, Auggie waits for me, where he will make love to me, and then sleep next to me until morning. Sometimes Auggie forces Rob to watch, and much to my dismay, once in a while he allows Rob to join. Not that Robin isn't a good lover. Truthfully, Rob rivals Auggie in prowess. It's a pair of distraught lovers that makes it difficult for me emotionally. I can handle one, but I never know if I'm going to get a pair or not.

The psychologist in me gets off on the cerebral fucking, while the woman in me wants to hug both Auggie and Rob, and then go apologize to Isis. Following that, I want to set the trio of them down for a thorough therapy session with a whole helluva lot of analyzing.

I think I'm going to be sick just thinking about it.

Duty calls, sliding off my stool, "See ya next week, Matt."

"Same time, same place," is his reply as I zigzag away.

Stumbling less than ten feet, more or less, I start giggling, realizing I've toppled over tipsy and officially entered into drunk as a skunk territory. "Whoa…" Bright-eyed and bushy-tailed, I teeter on wobbly legs. "I need to build up my tolerance," I shout back to Matt, who can drain a bottle and not even appear lit at all.

"Don't go there, girl," Matt warns me. Thinking he's going to impart some 'use me as an example as to why you shouldn't drink' advice, he says, "It's cheaper, the less tolerance you've got."

Laughing at myself, I fall to my ass, arms pin-wheeling and legs sprawling. I show a few of the writhing girls on the dance floor my Hello Kitty skivvies. Worried I'll gain attention from their adoring fans (drunk, horny FCC males looking for easy prey), they start gyrating even sluttier, hips thrusting at odd angles and asses almost touching the floor as they show how low… low… low… they can go.

"Little Pup, you're not driving home," comes from far above me. I look up, and up, and up, to find Rory standing over me. Looking disapproving yet amused, he shakes his head at me sadly.

Giggling, too drunk to feel ashamed, "If you expect me to argue, I'm not gonna. I can't even stand." Flopping backward onto the dirty floor, I slur, "You look funny from this angle."

"Funny ha-ha, or funny strange?" Rory asks, refusing to help me up until I answer.

Uninhibited, "Funny hot," I slur but it comes out sounding seductive to my schnapps-seduced ears. I blush bright red while laughing at myself.

Reaching down to pull me to my feet, Rory says, "I'll take funny hot, I guess. Up we go," he warns in a sing-song voice.

Imitating the Geico Piggy, "Wee… wee… wee…," I squeal as Rory picks me up to carry me out to the parking lot, and I don't even care that I'm now flashing those Hello Kitty skivvies to anyone who takes a look at my ass. Rory's rumbling laughter is accompanied by several of Rush's patrons.

Rory, singing with me, "All the way home."

CHAPTER THREE

"Please, for the love of all that is holy, do NOT say *wee* one more time," Rory demands in a strained voice. "And get your head back inside the window before a sign takes it out. You are *not* a piggy."

Hanging halfway out the passenger side window, "Wee…" I breathe into the wind, and then slide back into the car. Rory just shakes his head at me while I find myself the most hilarious thing I've ever seen or heard. "Wee…"

"I'm cutting you off. No more drinkies for you, chickapoo. You're fucking cute, I'll give you that." Eyes darting from the road to me, back to the road, back to me. "Too cute," Rory mumbles, fingers clenching on the steering wheel. "Where am I taking you? Are you still living at home, or do you have your own place?"

"Tomorrow, I'm looking for my own place," I reveal, talkative enough to spill my deepest, darkest secrets. "Essie and I are looking for places. I just paid for my last semester. That is, if signing more loan documents, and begging for more student aid and scholarships counts as paying. I'm dirt poor but education rich… poorer than dirt poor."

"Still living at home, I take it," Rory says wryly since I never truly answered him. "Your parents are going to kill me when I drag you through the house, meaning *my* parents are going to kill me when yours rat my ass out for intoxicating their only child."

"Wee…"

"Bethany!" Rory barks, getting annoyed with my drunk ass.

Spilling my deepest, darkest, "You should take me to the Spook House. I have some more payments I have to make… and I'm in the perfect mood for it."

"Ugh," a sharp grunt is pulled from my throat as my head meets the dashboard abruptly. Foggy, "Did we just get into an accident?" slurs as I rub my forehead with the heel of my palm. I turn to look at Rory, making sure he's okay, and find a seething man staring back at me. "What? Why are we stopped in the middle of the road?"

"Explain," Rory demands. When I don't answer right away, "Payments? As in whoring? Or did you mean you were in the mood for sex?" His voice is rising louder with every word spoken.

"Uh… um… I meant my Playroom dues," I tell the truth, but not the whole truth. "I'm drunk, so therefore, I am horny. Par for the course, as they say."

Glacial blue eyes glaring at me, "Let me get this straight. You won't go on a date with me until you graduate, but you'll fuck in the Playroom?"

"Just Auggie," pops out before I can stop it. "I've only ever been with Auggie, with a little side of Rob every once and a while."

Sounding mystified yet pained, "Why?" Rory breathes, clearly disappointed in the little girl he still sees me as.

Unable and unwilling to divulge my secrets, I evade Rory's question. "Ask me again when I'm sober," I say sheepishly. My liquid courage is lessening. Changing the subject, "Don't worry. Mom and Dad won't know you brought me home. I live in a tiny apartment over the garage. Plus, it's not like you got me drunk. You're just being a nice guy."

"Nice guy?" Rory looks even angrier as he turns away from me. Driving again, he threatens beneath his breath, "We'll just see about that."

vroom vroom

This man was built for hard, laborious work. With me swung over Rory's muscular shoulder like a sack of drunk potatoes, he climbs a steep flight of outside stairs without breaking a sweat, but his breath is elevated– has been since he stopped the car in the middle of the street five minutes ago. I can tell Rory is furious with me by his silence and taut muscles, but he is gentle with me otherwise.

I reach out and twist my unlocked doorknob, which elicits a groan of disapproval from Rory's throat. But otherwise he doesn't mention how stupid it is for a young woman not to lock her home, even if it's only for a few hours. Kicking the door to swing open, Rory deposits me inside my home, manhandling me with displeasure but with absolutely no unnecessary roughness.

"There's nothing to steal," I rumble, uncomfortable with Rory's cool assessment of my home. I can practically feel the judgment wafting from him.

Roughly, like it physically pains him to say the words, "But there is someone to harm."

"Oh." I sigh, feeling like a naïve, too stupid to live heroine from a romance novel. "I'm dumb."

"That you are, but you're usually not quite so stupid... and you call this a tiny apartment," Rory complains as he abruptly drops my ass onto my bed, causing me to shriek with surprise. Angrily gesturing around my space, "I could shit in your toilet, with one hand in the sink and one in the fridge, with my feet on your midget bed, all the while watching TV. Are you serious? This isn't a garage. It's a fucking shed!"

Insulted beyond belief, but more so hurt that Rory is disappointed in me, I fire back at him. "Don't be rude, mister!" I shift on my twin-sized bed and start peeling off my dress. "Why do you think I'm looking for a new place? I'm almost twenty-two, I didn't want to live in the house with my parents. I'm just happy Dave Prynne installed me some plumbing."

"Girls are idiots," Rory grumbles, all the while he wanders around my '*apartment*'. I live above our two-car garage, so it is rather small. I have a hot water tank, a toilet, a sink, and shower on one wall. A twin-sized bed with my dresser butted up against the footboard with my television sitting on top of it. My mini-fridge is my nightstand, and it's holding my Hello Kitty microwave.

All the Hello Kitty shit Essie bought for me as a joke, saying puppies and kittens didn't get along. Essie wanted me to be a cat instead of a dog during my thesis quest. The animal fetish was Essie's idea, but I vetoed the kitten in favor of the puppy when she wanted me to literally dress up as Hello Kitty. My best friend is batshit cray-cray, with too high of a limit on her Target Card. If Essie has a girl, I'm giving all the girly stuff back for the baby to have in her room.

"It's cozy," I giggle, being utterly ridiculous. "It's like a tight, little nest."

Glacial blue eyes flicking in my direction, "What do you buy with your money?" Sounding incredulous and disappointed, Rory fingers my stacks and stacks of Blu-rays, inspecting the titles with censure.

Drunk. Worried. Sad. Pitiful. I kneel in the middle of my bed with my dress half hanging off my body. "Those were gifts from my friends, trying to be nice to me, 'cuz they know I like my shows." I try not to whine or pout, but the booze brings it out of me. Plus, I hate how disappointed Rory looks at me, like he's judging me for being a dipshit girl.

I can't have my dream man seeing me as a flighty chick, so I go on the defensive. "My parents aren't rich. Hell, they aren't even comfortable, so I'm not going to tax their asses with my needs. So I got my cosmetology license so I could have a real job while I went to school. Minimum wage wasn't going to cut it with all my tuition costs. I've been working my ass off since I was seventeen, doing a double course load while holding a fulltime job. I found out the hard way that the salon pays jack, so I had to make a decision between a car and insurance or rent. If I chose the rent, eating was out of the question. I'm being pragmatic."

The sound of my cell phone ringing cuts into any response Rory might have had. I scramble to reach for it where it lies on the foot of my bed, but Rory is faster. Phone unlocked and pressed to his ear in less than a second, he doesn't speak, doesn't even say hello.

"Bethany can't come out and play with you this evening, Auggie," words cordial, voice feral. "No, I will not speak to you as if you are my boss. You aren't my boss." Eyes narrowing with annoyance, "Because I refuse to 'yes, sir' my high school buddy, that's why. Isis didn't play ball with me, she told me what to do. Isis is also the person who owns Rush, whether the deed is in her name or not. Isis is *my* boss," he stresses.

My eyebrows pop up in silent question, wondering about this odd conversation Auggie and Rory are having.

"You can threaten to fire me, yet again, just like the other thousand times. But I will continue to come into work as long as Isis will have me. Since it's been Isis and me running your fucking club since it opened, I'd stop this macho-posturing-bullshit if I were you. You have no leverage on me. So no, I'm not dragging Bethany's drunk pussy to your bed, you disrespectful fuck." Heavy pause where Rory looks murderous, eyes glaring, large fist clenched at his side.

"No, I am not 'using' your mistress this evening. Bethany had too much to drink, probably because she didn't want to service you, your highness." Rory glares at me so piercingly that

I cower on my bed. "Whatever the fuck you're doing with Bethany, it's done," Rory says with finality as he hangs up on his boss, causing my heart to beat into overdrive.

"Rory, no," I cry in a panic, seeing my future aspirations dissolve before my very eyes. Rory's reaction is exactly why we can't date until my thesis is completed.

Softly placing my cellphone on my dresser, Rory won't look me in the eye. "I don't get you, Bethany," he whispers, voice thick with emotion. At a loss, he just shakes his head over and over. "You were always smart. With how busy you are, why the Playroom? Why fuck around with Auggie? It's not like you to be this way."

Choking on a plethora of intense emotions, both in Rory's voice and written across his features, and within my heart, I nearly suffocate. "Ask me again when I'm sober," I repeat, not wanting to say too much in my semi-inebriated state of being.

"That conversation will be sooner rather than later." Rory doesn't threaten– it's a warning of a promise that will be met.

I go on the defensive, using distraction to avoid a long-overdue conversation. After nearly a year of wandering around naked while performing tricks as if I was a puppy, and occasionally having sex with witnesses, I have absolutely no modesty. Plus, the woman inside me, who is in love with Rory Essex, wants to get a reaction out of the man in question. Rory can blame it on the schnapps, when in actuality, drunk or sober, I still would have stripped bare-assed naked in front of him without any qualms.

As a teenager, when Rory would visit his parents during the summer months, I made sure I was wearing an itty-bitty bikini, a great tan, and a big smile. Since Rory's visits were sporadic, I was always wearing a bikini. As for the tan, since I had to sit in my front lawn waiting for my prince charming to arrive, let's just say I hope I don't get premature aging from just how tan I would get every summer.

Mouth gaping open, Rory stands near the side of my bed, not that there is room to stand elsewhere in my apartment. "You're not little Bethany Oman from next door any longer," he drawls out in appreciation, voice husky and thready.

I know I'm not perfect, but I know without a shadow of a doubt that I'm perfect for Rory Essex– always knew I was. I felt it in my soul since the first day we met.

I'm not arrogant. I'm confident. I'm a young woman with a womanly body: a little too much curve to my belly, too much wiggle-waggle to my thighs, too much jiggle-jaggle in my trunk, with too much sag to my breasts. My mom is a bigger woman, showing what I will undoubtedly become after I have children of my own. But after being in the Playroom with women in all shapes and sizes up to the age of eighty, I find every body shape beautiful. It's the confidence they exude that makes the true difference. I am nothing if not confident in my mind, body, and spirit, especially when it comes to Rory Essex.

"When I'm sober, you can ask me why I won't date you, and I'll tell you the God's honest truth. Ask me why I go to the Playroom, and you'll find that it's connected. But tonight, I'm not sober. So give me a kiss before you go, and I promise I won't shove you away. In fact, I'll kiss you back."

Face filled with agonizing torture, Rory gazes down at me like he's starving. Uninhibited, shameless, I arch my back against my mattress, opening my thighs to his homing gaze, cool air caressing and kissing at my lust-swollen, moist flesh. At the sight of my salaciousness, a pain-filled groan is torn from Rory's throat.

"Christ! You're perfect," Rory tells me something I already know. "Shit," he hisses, looking even more tortured. "You're wet. But are you wet for me, or for the man I just hung up on? Are you horny drunk?"

Snorting, smirking, "Horny drunk?" I ask, sounding incredulous. "This coming from the man who has run in the opposite direction from me since I was a hormone-crazed thirteen-year-old girl? What do you think?"

Neck straining, eyes glued to the flesh between my thighs, bulge growing impossibly large behind the denim of his jeans, Rory looks pained. "Trust me, Beth, it was for your own good. You were a little girl, and I had very grown up thoughts about your horny, tiny body."

Hand brushing down my stomach, fingers slipping between my thighs, slipping between my moist lips. My body jerks as I make contact with my throbbing clit. "Not a little girl anymore... not so tiny either," I say in a voice that sounds drugged with lust and hunger. Eyes flicking to land on his huge package, awed, "And neither are you, mister. My God, you must be fucking hung."

Grumbling uncomfortably, "I'm proportionate." Blushing. Rory has an honest to God blush riding high on his cheeks, and it's slowly creeping down his neck. The sight turns me on even more, and I don't even realize I'm still touching myself for him, fingers fluttering over my needy flesh.

Like the Evil Queen with the temptation of a red, juicy apple, my fingertips extend in Rory's direction, salaciously offering my sweet cream to him. "Taste," I demand in a lusty, coaxing cadence, knowing if Rory tastes I will have him for the rest of my evening. My thighs part farther, offering another option for his dining pleasure– fingertips or pussy.

My mouth waters, imagining how Rory would taste coating my tongue, sliding down the back of my throat to nourish my belly. I lick my lips, starving, anticipating the moment he slips deep inside my mouth… my pussy.

Leaning toward me before he realizes, looking mesmerized by the glossy shine on my fingertips, Rory's eyes widen in alarm. Quickly righting himself, he puts as much distance between us as my tiny apartment will allow.

"Kiss me," I beg in a deep, throaty voice filled with ache. My legs scissor on the mattress, fueled by the burning need between my thighs. Every inch of my body craves every inch of Rory's flesh.

Eyes closed, refusing to look at me. "Beth," Rory breathes out between clenched teeth, clearly sexually frustrated. "I'm trying to be an honorable man, here. But you're making it very difficult. I don't want you to be pissed tomorrow when you wake up, and somehow blame it on me."

Posing on my bed while wearing nothing but a naughty, enticing smirk, "I'm not *that* drunk, Rory."

Turning away from me, Rory surprises me when he opens my door to leave. Rory speaks to me over his shoulder, but still doesn't look at me. "But I am not *that* stupid, Bethany. I refuse to do anything to fuck this up." Voice gravelly with promise, "I've waited a lifetime for you," he confesses. He walks out of my apartment, and then shuts the door behind him.

The '*I've waited a lifetime for you*' was all I needed to hear. "R-O-R-Y! E-S-S-E-X!" I shout, frustrated. "I don't need honorable. I just need you! Get back in here!"

Sliding beneath my Hello Kitty sheets, I swear I hear Rory's satisfied laugher rumbling in the distance as he jogs down the steps from my apartment to the driveway.

"Have fun walking back to Rush!" I shout to the slowly fading laughter.

CHAPTER FOUR

Dead tired, hung over, and annoyed, is not a good combination when making life-altering decisions over rental agreements with skeevy landlords, especially in this shit area of Fairport. Standing on the sidewalk, Essie and I try not to look too closely at our surroundings. My pregnant best friend keeps squirting hand sanitizer into our palms.

In the yard across the street, a haggard woman with four kids under the age of five is screaming bloody murder but never lifting a hand to make her children behave. "Stop hitting your sister, Billy!" she shouts, all the while watching her largest child beat the ever-loving hell out of her smallest daughter. God forbid she uses the good sense He gave her and actually intervenes. But I guess it's too much effort to get off her cellphone for five seconds and yank the bully off the little girl who's wailing in pain.

"MOMMA!" the middle kid shrieks to get her attention, but is otherwise ignored. Finally, three of the kids gang up on the bully, saving their baby sister.

"If we have to live here," Essie whispers into my ear, "That woman is going to have a Prynne-style attitude adjustment."

"I'll be on hold with CPS," I offer a better, less bloodthirsty solution.

"It's $750.00 a month," the fortyish skeevy landlord with the porn-stache demands the second he walks up to us on the sidewalk. He even puts his palm out like we're just going to slap the money in it, apartment sight-unseen.

Saying exaggeratedly while making a funny gesture with my hands, "Plus?"

"Plus nuttin'," the Ron Jeremy wannabe grunts out. "That's first, last, and security. I'll need $2,250 before I even think of holding the place. I'm a busy man, so if you want it, ya better take it now. I've got lots of people calling, and I'm sure you've noticed, there ain't much available in Fairport these days. Economy's bad, so they're staying put like rats. Only reason this apartment is free is because I had to evict the deadbeat."

"How much was the deadbeat's rent?" Essie mouths to me.

Johnny Wadd has sonic hearing, "Five hundred. Inflation."

"Yeah, well, my wages ain't inflatin'," Essie mimics the douche-noodle's diction. "My wages are the same as when these shitholes were going for three hundred a month, not the astronomical amount you're asking. Meanwhile, my tips are going down because of assholes like you sucking the rest of us dry."

"Insult me all ya want, fuck if I care." Looking put out, he gestures to himself, "Do I look rich to you?" Wearing a short-sleeved plaid shirt with all the buttons undone– tucking the shirt into his jorts is the only reason it's not gaping open enough to show off his pot gut and belly button. The man is not rich, unless an abundance of wiry chest hair is currency. "I ain't eating no profits. My property taxes keep going up and up, and the cocksucking insurances. Alot," he says as one word, driving me batshit crazy.

"Fuck me." Essie sighs, already sounding defeated. "Let's take a look."

"You girls go on up. I'll stay here," he says while getting comfortable by leaning on the outside of the building. "Don't take nuttin'," he warns.

"Take what?" Essie pulls out her Prynne attitude. "The motherfucking light bulbs?"

"Nah, those are already gone. Last asshole took every bulb in the place, along with all the switch plate covers."

Arching a brow in question, "You replaced them, right?" I sigh heavily when the landlord just looks at me. "Of course, you didn't."

"Well, if I strap the fridge on my back and carry it down here, will you help me put it on top of my Toyota?" Essie taunts, looking like a teacup-sized pregnant woman who is mimicking a badassed mofo.

I don't know which I want to laugh at more as they banter back and forth, Essie or the slum lord.

"No fridge," he grunts. "Last tenant took that, too... and the stove."

"There's a toilet, right?" I sound sarcastic, but I'm not. "There better fucking be, asswipe," I warn as I leave the slum landlord to hold up the side of his dilapidated building.

"You sure this place isn't condemned?" Essie whispers to me as we traverse the flight of piss-stank stairs.

"No, I'm pretty sure it is. But at least there is a front door. The last place didn't have any doors, remember? And that trailer, where we showed up and it was a 'shared' unit with another family."

"I took pictures of that gem for Facebook." Essie giggles. "It had pink wall-to-wall shag carpeting."

"Not hard to do when the walls are only eleven feet apart," I grumble. "And filled with nine people."

Good humor deflating, Essie looks petrified and heartbroken. "I'm going to be homeless, I just know it. Seven hundred and fifty bucks is too much. I could swing maybe, three hundred. Unless we find a third, I doubt we can rent anywhere."

"We'll figure something out," I try to sound more hopeful than I feel. I yank Essie into the apartment, "C'mon. Let's have a look."

"Ugh," Essie sneers, retching a little when the stench hits us directly in the face, a mix of cat piss and rotten garbage juice that draws her morning sickness. "Can we not look and just say we did?"

"This is the last place available in town, and skeevy McGee wasn't joking. His bread will be buttered by someone," I mutter in disgust.

"I'd rather not butter that vile man's bread." Essie visibly shudders. "I can't do this to you, Beth. Your place is small, but it's free. You have your privacy. Only reason we're doing this is because I'm gonna be homeless. In a few months, I won't be able to work as much, putting more of a strain on you." Tugging my hand, "C'mon, let's leave. I'll figure something out."

"We'll be fine," I say again, still not believing it.

Entering the one bedroom apartment, we gaze around in abject horror. It's one large room with peeling paint and torn and scuffed linoleum flooring, with two doors leading to the bedroom and bathroom. No stove. No fridge. Looks like we'll be eating from Hello Kitty the microwave and my mini-fridge, just as I am now.

"This is big enough for you to take the bedroom," I say to Essie as I try to look at the positives. "My bed will fit well in that corner over there. You'll need the room to yourself for when the baby is born."

"No," Essie denies, shaking her head. She tries to pull me out of the apartment again, while she rambles on, like she's giving me a sales pitch. "You need to keep your ass at home. As soon as you graduate, your loans are gonna be due. I can't burden you like this. You should be saving up to pay off your debts, dating Rory, and maybe splitting his rent... if Rory even pays rent living at Rush. I doubt he does, and I bet his place is really nice. You know how anal Isis is about everything."

"Rory's a nonissue," I lie only to myself since I know Essie sees right through my bullshit. "I. Will. Not. Strand. You." I give Essie a little shake. "Devon should have to pay you some support or something for his kid in your gut. Breastfeeding for a year or not, without a roof over its head and diapers on its ass, it's neglect."

"Good luck finding Devon." Essie tries to sound nonplussed, but she is in some serious pain. Devon is to Essie as Rory is to me. I feel sick to my stomach every time I think about it. I envision Rory knocking me up after a one-night-stand, and then calling *me* the worthless, irresponsible whore for sleeping with him... I was there, and it was all Devon's doing. It breaks my heart just thinking about it. If I could ever find the spineless cocksucker, I'd de-nut him.

"I'm sure Devon is in this slum of a building, or the landlord is holing Dev up somewhere. This looks like a great place to get high," I try for teasing, but it comes out seething.

"No doubt the tenants need to get high just to live in this shithole," Essie grumbles. "Let's go, dammit. I can't take this shit any longer. The smell alone is bringing on my morning sickness."

Being dragged down a flight of stairs to the outside of the building, I sound out of breath. "When are your parents leaving?"

"Yesterday," is Essie's startling reply.

Pulling Essie to a stop near the lurking landlord, "You're joking, right?"

"No, I wish I was," is her exhausted reply. "I've got less than a week before the new buyers take over the house. Mom and Dad shoved my shit into Uncle Dave's garage."

Turning to the sleazeball, "We'll be back in the morning, with the cash. If you get rid of it beforehand, I guess it wasn't meant to be."

Smiling creepily, with dollar signs flashing in his eyes, "Ten a.m., and don't be late."

CHAPTER FIVE

My original plan for my thesis was to dissect the different reasons the patrons of the Playroom visited, but over time it evolved into an in-depth look inside Augustus Kline's psyche. Auggie is as complex as one can be, with layers upon layers of emotional wounds that affect his actions on a daily basis. The man has all these rules he lives by, rules that seem to contradict his behavior and get in the way of his own happiness. So as I write my thesis, I realize Auggie sees himself as a whore. As if not good enough for the people he loves, for the family he belongs. Auggie holds himself just far enough apart not to get sucked into their unconditional love.

Augustus Kline: Reigning supreme within a deviant kingdom of his own creation, by Bethany Oman. Pg. 276

Born to a drug addict teenage runaway and an unnamed father, Augustus Kline's view on women is tainted by the actions of his mother and baby sister, seeing them as worthless, unnecessary outside of the bedroom and child-rearing. A view that was solidified by the only male, fatherly influence in his young life: John Mason, deceased. For Augustus Kline, there are two types of women: wives and whores, and the twain shall never intersect.

In contradiction to Augustus Kline's misogynistic, slightly bent view on women, both of his businesses are run by women, leaving them with the bulk of the responsibility. On course with his core beliefs, neither woman is allowed in his bed, no matter how much he wishes them to visit it. In Augustus Kline's view, both Isis Mason and Willow Prynne are untouchable, wives in waiting. To engage them in his bedroom is to render them whores.

Augustus Kline longs for a normal life, the kind with a house, picket fence, two-point-five children, and a yellow lab named Max. As the bastard son of a whore, Auggie struggles with his own self-worth, mixed with the fact that what he longs to have contradicts with what will truly make him happy. Bisexual, in love with both a man and woman, Augustus Kline is a lost soul— the founding member of his very own lost souls club.

The Playroom.

"Damn," drawls from next to my shoulder, causing me to jump out of my skin while releasing a very girly squeak. "Does Auggie know he's your subject?" Rory muses, large palm settling on my shoulder to soothe my speeding heartbeat.

Craning my head backward to look up at Rory, "You scared the shit out of me," I admit breathlessly. "I almost peed my pants."

"You're not wearing any pants," Rory teases, plucking at my Hello Kitty nightshirt. Like an expert in Microsoft Office, he reaches forward to press CTRL + S to save my thesis. "As for scaring the shit out of you, lock your goddamned door, won't you? Whether you are in this hole of an apartment or not, lock it," he bites, shutting my laptop.

"Yes, master," I say with little to no respect, not planning on locking my door since the lock is broken and I've yet to replace it. In actuality, it's never been locked in my entire life. "I'm guessing you're here to talk since I'm now sober."

Flashing me a '*no shit*' look, "Whatever gave you that idea?" Rory sits on my twin-sized bed, and then tugs my desk chair until I'm sitting directly in front of him. Fearing he's going to start interrogating me, he surprises me with, "What's up with all the kid shit in here?"

Snorting, smirking, I smother the need to laugh at the ridiculousness of the situation. My God, mammoth Rory Essex is sitting on my teeny-tiny bed amongst a plethora of Hello Kitty paraphernalia. It only took seventeen years for such an occurrence.

Be still my beating heart.

I'm all aflutter.

I may swoon.

Crystalline blue eyes shining with amusement, Rory chuckles, dimples indenting his pretty cheeks, no doubt knowing I'm making fun of him in my private thoughts.

"It started out as a joke from Essie, teasing me about how kittens and puppies don't get along. Then my mother walked in here, seeing all of the Hello Kitty bullshit, and assumed she found something I would love. The woman is a great mom, trying to please me and make me feel loved. So after that, every holiday and everyday thinking-of-you gift has been Hello Kitty related. Mom and Essie have everyone I know buying me this shit."

Lips curling up at the corners into a private smirk, Rory looks at me like he knows me better than anyone. "...and you hate Hello Kitty."

Emphatically agreeing, "... and I *hate* Hello Kitty."

Laughing with each other, both of our eyes are magnetized to the other's lips. Happy sounds drying up, leaving behind strained silence, we both wait for the other to speak first. Reminiscent of years of staring contests and battles-of-will, it's as comforting as it is frustrating.

As always, I break first.

Truth spills from my lips, but undoubtedly it's not the truth Rory is seeking. "Essie and I found an apartment today that neither of us can afford, even combining our funds. I don't want to live there. I don't want her to live there. I wouldn't raise a child there if my life depended on it." I admit for the first time that I don't have a plan, and I hate it. Since I was a freshman in high school, I've always known what path to take. "I have no idea what to do."

"Bethany." Rory sighs, reaching forward to hold my hand. "Essie is your best friend, I get that. I have friends too, and I wouldn't let them down for anything. But Essie has a family who can take care of her, and there is no way in hell Malcolm wouldn't support the girl and his grandchild. You get that, don't you?"

"Are you sure?" I sound so hopeful, needing to believe Rory because I cannot in good conscience ever step foot into that God awful apartment ever again.

"I'm positive. You're just starting out in life, and right now you need to be selfish and worry about yourself. Essie needs to concentrate on herself as well. You know her family well, do they seem like they would toss her on the street?"

"No. I understand Essie's need to feel independent, not to live with her family. It's why I'm in this shed as if I'm a responsible adult living on her own, when in reality I'm still under my parents' roof, even if I'm in another building." Feeling down on myself, feeling badly for Essie, depression settles over me like a too-hot blanket on a warm summer night.

Scooting my chair forward, Rory widens his legs until I am nestled between them. His heavy palm meets the back of my head, pulling me forward until I'm resting my cheek against his broad chest.

Whispering against my hair, "Tell me what you want, Bethany, and I'll do my damnedest to give it to you."

The combination of his sincerity, his lulling voice, his warm scent, I tell Rory what he wants to know. "I want to feel like a grown woman, not live with my parents. I don't want to feel as if I'm not only treading water but being sucked backward upstream. No matter what I do, it feels like I can't get ahead. I work a dead-end career that required a degree, and I barely make enough money to pay my car payment. In a few months, my debts will be due, and I have no idea how I will afford almost a hundred grand in student loans. It may have only taken me four and a half years, but I still owe for a Master's degree."

Hands slowly rubbing my back, Rory tries to reassure me. "I have little doubt that you will do well in your career, and eventually you will pay back your debts."

"I see a lot of Ramen in my future," I mutter sarcastically. "My parents may get sick of paying for the extra utilities on this place, and for the internet and cable I scab from them every month... and for the Ramen I swipe from their cupboards."

Chest rumbling beneath my cheek, Rory quietly laughs with me, or *at* me. "I get that you want your own place, right? So why are you avoiding me, Bethany?" Pressure mounting. "You and I want the exact same thing, but for some reason you are delaying the inevitable. I could help you now when you need it the most, and you and I could help each other for the rest of our lives. Why are you waiting until you graduate? Don't you know I want what's best for you? I'd give you anything you'd ever want or need. I'd never stop you from chasing your dreams. Fuck, I'd chase them with you, just for the pleasure of seeing your face when you finally reach your goal."

"Oh, Rory," I whimper, pressing my face against his chest to stem the need to cry. "I've wanted you since long before I even knew what it meant to want someone. But I can't... just not yet."

Simply, "Why?"

No judgment. No disappointment. Rory is being sincere, as if the answer to his question is the most important thing in his world, which is exactly why I answer him truthfully.

"You read that page of my thesis from over my shoulder, I know you did. You get that I'm analyzing Auggie, and I have to be in the Playroom. Auggie is my protector, and I have certain tolls I must pay for that protection. Tolls that a boyfriend could never handle. Tolls that would make me unfaithful, and my conscience wouldn't be able to handle it."

Voice even, formal, as if Rory is trying to hide his true feelings on the subject. "Do you need to sleep with Auggie to remain in the Playroom?"

"No," I admit the truth. "I have to sleep with Auggie for my own protection. I do and don't regret it, but it's better than having a bunch of guys trying to touch me. Auggie just tells them to get the fuck away from me and they listen."

Cautious, "So this is what's holding you back from me? Your degree is contingent on the Playroom, which means in order for you to be safe in the Playroom, you have to sleep with Auggie? But you can't date me because you'd feel guilty for touching another man if you were with me?"

"Exactly," I breathe in relief, glad the truth is out in the open so I don't have to lie anymore.

Squeezing me tightly, "My Bethany," rolls off Rory's tongue like a caress. "She wants a place to call her own, to feel like a real woman. I can give her that," he says to himself with conviction. "I can also give her a better paying job since she is unhappy with her current financial situation. Rush can't keep an assistant because they're scared of Isis, causing me to have to do all that office shit myself. I'm sure the bazillion years of schooling prepared her for answering emails, calling vendors, and running to the post office. Isis is asleep during normal business hours, and I'd like to be as well."

"You're giving me a job?" sounding highly incredulous, knowing it's a made-up job to give me some extra cash.

"And a home," Rory says, sounding amused, like he knows exactly what I was thinking. "Rent-free, all utilities included, even cable, internet, and Netflix. Isis and I just make Auggie pay for it, stating we're one household since we share Rush's address... well, we only share one wall to our lofts, but who's going to check."

"Auggie ought to," I say wryly.

"Auggie's lazy," Rory grits, voicing an underlying resentment for his absentee boss.

"All that sounds good, six months from now. Because you're forgetting one vital thing, Rory." I breathe, trying to keep my voice even, "The Playroom."

"Well, I shall join the Playroom and protect you," Rory sounds so sure of himself that I burst out laughing.

Pulling away from Rory's warm, comforting embrace, I roll on the casters of my desk chair, putting some much-needed space between us. "Ain't happening, cowboy," I drawl, amused yet mortified for Rory if he plans on approaching Auggie with his lunacy. "Ain't. Gonna. Happen. No way. No how."

As serious as I've ever seen him, Rory looks me in the eyes and professes, "I'll do anything for you, Bethany. Anything. I'll go through Auggie if I must."

Awed. Gobsmacked. I just shake my head back in forth in wonderment. "You have no idea what you're saying. Auggie's toll is way too high. I'm fucking him twice a month for protection, and that is *after* I paid the toll to enter the Playroom. Auggie's toll for the guys is a lot higher than I've ever paid."

"I can handle it," Rory bites, looking as if I'm insulting him as a man.

"Prove it," I challenge, rolling back a bit farther to give him room to stand between me and the bed. "Whip your dick out and let me see it."

Sputtering, coughing, Rory's aghast expression is priceless. "What?" he squawks.

"If doing that for me is difficult, then you don't have a chance in hell of getting into the Playroom," I warn.

"Fine," Rory bites, but the naughty glimmer in his blue eyes informs me he wants me to see him in all of his glory. "You've been trying to get into my pants since you were a kid," he teases me. "I guess now is as good a time as any."

Hand on his zipper, Rory breathes deeply, closing his eyes, like he's heavily concentrating on something. "What are you doing?" I laugh.

"Arousing myself," he says without shame. "Like I'm gonna let you see me flaccid." Smirking at me, "… Okay, I'm good."

"Do I even want to know what you were imagining?" Laughter dying on my lips, my eyes bulge from my skull when Rory's dick flops out of his jeans. "Holy. Fuck. That's a thick cock…" Jutting proudly from his fly, Rory's cock is competition for Auggie's Beast. Nowhere near as long, probably not much longer than average. "Does your hand even fit around that thing?" I gesture at his mammoth cock.

"Of course," he says, smile thick in his voice. Proving himself wrong, Rory's fingertips do NOT touch when he grips his dick.

I close my eye against the insane need to stroke and lick and suck and bite and swallow that impressive length of thick flesh. I have no doubt that Rory has never had a good blowjob, and I fear I will never be able to handle the girth of his dick in my mouth.

"Rory," I say in warning. "You won't get into the Playroom."

Furious, Rory tucks his erection back into his jeans, having a difficult time closing his pants around it. "Wanna bet?" he challenges me.

"Sure," I mutter, sad that I have to wait six more months for my dream future after Rory dangled it before me. (Not his cock, you perverts! His heart and home). Six more months of servicing Auggie's girlfriend fantasies. Six more months of living in stasis.

Stepping around me, Rory makes his way toward my door. He turns around and points at me. "When I get into the Playroom, you will immediately owe me twenty-four hours where you will do everything and anything I say without question. Fair enough?"

"Fair enough," I agree, feeling confident that I will not have to pay up on our wager. "If you don't, then you will patiently wait out the next six months without pressuring me."

Looking disappointed in me, "You doubt me," he says in a stiff voice.

"No, you underestimate Auggie's deviancy," I say in warning.

"I'll be back, and when I get here, you better be packed and ready to do whatever I say. First order of business, last night was the last night you will sleep in a 'room' without a proper lock. Last night was the last night you will sleep without me. From now on, it's you and me, Bethany. Mark my words." Exiting my 'room', Rory declares ominously, "Mark. My. Words."

A shiver of trepidation makes its way up my spine. I don't know which I fear more, Rory failing... or succeeding.

CHAPTER SIX

Rory Essex

Determination pushes me forward, no thought of surrender. Panting wildly, I can't control my reaction to what I'm about to do. I trust Auggie with my life. I respect him as a friend. I know he will never physically harm me. With that saying, I also understand his perversions. So I know whatever this toll may be, it's going to have a very steep price.

I met Auggie Kline on my first day of freshman year. He was my personal welcoming committee that was closer to a hazing. I was a big kid, almost a grown man at that age. But when Auggie strode up to me, I was shaking like a leaf. I had no idea why a senior guy would want to talk me.

"Us big dudes gotta stick together," was the first thing out of Auggie's mouth. "You're young yet, but someone has to teach you to control yourself. You could harm someone without even realizing it."

"I've never been in a fight," I admitted, blushing profusely like I should be ashamed for being a nice guy.

Nodding like he understood, Auggie grabbed my elbow, tugging me toward the football field. "Shit happens," he said with a shrug. "It's best to be prepared for the unexpected."

Entering the field, a smaller guy and a beautiful girl awaited us. They were sitting side-by-side, drawing on the soles of the guy's sneakers with a Sharpie. I stared in wonder, not at the kids but at the artwork– it was so realistic that I wanted to tell him to take his sneakers off and frame them.

Auggie smiled at them like they were sunshine to his darkness. "Rob and Isis," Auggie pointed out. "Reason why I had to learn to be gentle when I battle. Horseplay could end up breaking a bone if you're not careful. We don't realize our strength until it's too late."

The girl's laughter was low and seductive, scaring the shit out of me more so than Auggie's six-foot-four massive body. "He's always too gentle," she said, like it annoyed her. I swear the small guy named Rob sighed at her words, like he was exhausted by the thought.

Placing his large palms in the center of my chest, Auggie pushed me to the ground. I landed on my ass with a loud thump. "What the fuck, man?" I shouted, furious. Scrambling to my feet, I decided now was the best time to have my first fight.

"That was me controlling my strength," Auggie warned. "Don't make me use my full-force. Got it?" Angry but no longer confused, I just nodded in agreement. "Your turn," Auggie gestured for me to come at him. "Gimme all ya got so I can figure out how to teach you."

With a feral smirk, I muttered, "Gladly," as I charged Auggie with all my might. I felled Auggie like a tree in the forest, moving him a good ten feet and knocking his ass to the ground. Isis and Rob howled their approval, shouting like they were ringside at a wrestling match.

Fearing Auggie would be angry with me, I stepped back, out of his reach.

"Good God, kid," Auggie said in awe, eyes shining up at me with unexpected respect. "You ain't even full-grown yet. You're gonna be unstoppable." Arching back to his feet with the grace and finesse of a dancer, Auggie said, "Again, and this time don't fucking hold back... and remember, I'll never harm you."

At fifteen years old, I never would have guessed that that day would alter the path of my life, inescapably entangling me in their lives.

In the year that followed, I was their pet freshman. Rob was a nice guy who smiled constantly like he knew my deepest secrets. I was leery to hold a conversation with Rob, like he was ferreting away everything I said for future use. It took months for me to be comfortable in Isis's presence. I had to look past her beauty and allure to see the friend beneath. Auggie and I were combatants in every way possible. No matter what, we just rubbed the other the wrong way. Equal parts friendship, respect, and competition.

After their graduation, I finally took a deep breath, amazed at how suffocating their intensity could be. Short-lived, Auggie would randomly pull up out front of my house and tell me to get into his truck. The man was happy to have found someone who could sustain the full force of his powerful punches, and he was satisfied with the way my fists felt bruising his flesh.

Even before I graduated from high school, I had a full-time job for life at Rush. Isis and I had forged a professional relationship because her sexual intensity scared me versus enticed me, which suited all of us. I've been the trio's shadow for the past ten years, with Auggie and me butting heads on a daily basis.

Our history, and Auggie's *"I'll never harm you,"* are little comfort as I enter the Spook House, ready to beg my way into the Playroom.

Stalking into their living room, I catch Rob and Auggie unaware. "Do you honestly believe Willow doesn't know? C'mon, Rob." Auggie snorts, sounding like the girl they are gossiping about.

"No one is *that* daft," Rob stresses. "Willow knows. In less than thirty-six hours, the world will know, too."

I don't ask, because I know what they are talking about. Anyone over the age of nineteen knows what the fuck is brewing. Mary Prynne at age fifty was not pregnant, and then, all of a sudden, she had a newborn. The scandal was Fairport's juiciest gossip for years.

"Are you guys playing Connect Four?" I startle both of them, which is extremely satisfying under the circumstances. "Seriously? Connect Four, while gossiping about Willow?"

Ignoring me, Auggie is sitting on a fragile sofa, hovering over the Connect Four frame, deciding on his next move. Rob is kneeling on the other side of the coffee table, taking his turn.

Rob's warm brown eyes glare up at me, scowling. "What of it?" he mutters, thoroughly annoyed as he blocks Auggie's chance at an early win. "We like to play old school board games, too… as you know since we used to force you to play with us."

"Oh, I remember how much you hated to fuckin' lose, Rob." I try to keep the snarl out of my voice. My loyalties lie with Isis, and these fuckheads are faithless when it comes to Isis. Over the years, our truce has become as fragile as that antique sofa beneath Auggie's hulking ass.

Sighing heavily, already ascertaining his loss at Connect Four, Auggie leans back against the sofa cushions. "I assume Rory is here to discuss our mistress."

With a naughty grin, Rob drops his black disc down the frame, securing his win at Connect Four. Somehow he gained the manipulative powers of the entire Prynne clan, leaving the rest of them dafter than cat shit, "Discuss? Or reclaim?"

"Rory doesn't even have to answer that," Auggie says as he gets more comfortable on his throne-like hundred-year-old sofa. "I can feel the ire radiating off of him like an imminent storm."

Picking up his toys, Rob flashes me a grin, promising I'll hate him for whatever comes out of his mouth next. Rob is jealous of my friendship with Isis, and he takes every chance he can get to put me in my place. "Me thinks Rory hates how we've been fucking his puppy."

Snarling, I cross the entire span of the living room in the blink of an eye. A meaty fist shoves me back several feet. "Remember what I've taught you. Remember how I told you I learned the same exact thing so I didn't accidently kill Rob. Now you understand why that was so very important," Auggie stresses. Instead of looking at me, he's glaring Rob's ass down for being a bastard.

Unrepentant, "Rory proved me right," Rob says with a shrug. Pouting like it's an Olympic sport, "He's here to take our lover away."

Hand dropping from my chest, Auggie steps away, confident I won't kill his… whatever the hell Robin Prynne is to Augustus Kline. "We still have six more months to our agreement," Auggie says, sounding bored. "Come back then and we will renegotiate our terms."

"I have some new terms," I announce. "Let me in the Playroom, and I will take Bethany off your hands forever." My voice dips low, eliciting a threatening warning.

I drop my bomb, rendering everyone speechless… until Rob comes back to life. "Am I hearing shit?" Robin's eyes go wide with excitement. "Please tell me I'm not hearing shit. Rory didn't just say he wanted to join the Playroom, did he? Did he?" With both Rob and Auggie staring at me in shock, I don't know how to respond to that. "He. So. Fucking. Did," Rob mutters in awe as he walks toward me on his knees. "Holy fuck, there is a Santa Claus after all."

"Are you high?" I grunt, sidestepping Rob when he gets within inches of my thigh. Eyeing him boldly, "What is wrong with you?"

No longer sounding bored, Auggie is a mix of fury and confusion. "Unfortunately, Rob is probably higher than a kite. He thinks I don't know about his recreational habit, but he couldn't be more wrong."

Shamefaced, retreating as if struck, Rob slides into an armchair, trying to look invisible and not guilty. "I'm not high," Rob mouths to me. "Honest."

Ignoring Rob's antics, Auggie speaks directly to me. "Rory, word of advice. You do not belong in the Playroom. You've lived a life of normalcy, and you will continue to live this way for the rest of your life. Allow Bethany to finish out her thesis, and then whisk her away to be your wife."

"No," I say with an inner strength that no one can deny. Fisting my chest, thumping with every word, "This. Ends. Now."

Big brown eyes flicking back and forth, Rob watches us like an intriguing tennis match, but otherwise he stays silent. However, Auggie doesn't stay silent. "You won't like what it takes to enter the Playroom. No straight man ever does," he says in warning, sounding ominous.

Swallowing thickly, "Whatever it takes," I say, and I truly mean it. "Bethany will no longer use her body to advance her career. If she wants to share my bed, so be it. I'll do whatever I can to make sure she's happy."

"Aww," Rob breathes, and I swear I hear a sniffle. Going from sweet to evil, "Rory is so going to regret saying that."

Gesturing to me, "Drop trou," Auggie commands.

"That's all?" I say, utterly shocked. In theory, I know Auggie and Rob are bisexual, but I thought they were more into each other than other guys, and I know for a fact they love pussy as much as I do. "All you want to see is my cock?"

Auggie just stares at me, analyzing my reaction, while Rob laughs outright.

"Now I get why Bethany made me do this for her before I came over here," I mutter to myself as I pop the button on my jeans and begin to unzip.

"Oh, I highly doubt you understand what's actually going on here," Rob purrs, eyes glued to my crotch. "Unzip slowly, please." Freaked out, my jeans are yanked to my knees in less than a second. "Always works like a charm on every straight dude," Rob says arrogantly. "Tighty whities too…"

"Rob is such a tease." Auggie's voice is deeper than I've ever heard it, like Rob's bullshit is arousing him.

"I doubt I've ever experienced a creepier moment in my entire life," I mutter to myself as I tug my undershorts down my thighs. I close my eyes as air hits my groin.

"You're so going to regret saying that," Rob repeats, and then quietly snickers. "Whoa… please tell me you're a grower, not a show-er. Can you make it hard for us?"

Sputtering, my eyes fly wide open. "God, no! Are you fucking insane?"

Green eyes wide, Auggie just stares at my junk with his mouth gaping open. "Life has been kind to you, my friend. No doubt you're a grower."

"Can I take Rory's toll? P-L-E-A-S-E?" Rob begs, fingers clenching his thighs to keep himself in his chair.

"No," Auggie barks. "No."

Pouting, "No fair," Rob whines, looking crestfallen.

"Life isn't fair," Auggie responds to him. "Rory, you can zip up. We'll go up to the room we use with Beth. There is a symmetry to that, I believe."

Confused, I pull my jeans back up and tuck my junk back where it belongs. "Huh? Aren't we done? Am I a member of the Playroom?"

Rob and Auggie share a look, and then burst out laughing. "That was just a test to see what your toll would be." Auggie makes a purr-like sound in the back of his throat, scaring the hell out of me. Rising from the sofa, Auggie possessively curls his palm around my elbow. "Shall we?"

Jumping up from his chair, Rob blurts, "Can I watch?"

"NO!" Auggie and I shout in unison.

Whispering as Auggie and I leave the living room, "No fair," Rob pouts.

CHAPTER SEVEN

Rory Essex

Auggie gestures for me to walk into the darkened bedroom ahead of him– the only light coming from a small lamp on the nightstand. I enter reluctantly, the gravity of what is actually happening finally settles over me. Bethany warned me. Auggie warned me. Rob warned me with every word he spoke. No way would anyone be so adamant against this if it was just about brandishing my cock. Standing in a bedroom outfitted with antique furnishings, I realize I'm in way over my head.

Auggie leans against the door, hand reaching back to lock the old-fashioned lock with a skeleton key. The click doesn't make me flinch… but believe me, I wanted to. Eyes intensely focused on me, Auggie then palms the key, metal disappearing to parts unknown.

I'm trapped in a bedroom in the Spook House, the very room in which Auggie uses *my* Bethany. And I'm trapped with Augustus Kline after I just showed him my dick in his living room. Rob was indeed correct, this is now the creepiest moment of my entire life.

Severely serious, "I need honest answers," Auggie warns from his frozen position against the door.

"In ten years, I've never once lied to you, Auggie," I say with all sincerity.

Closing his eyes, Auggie looks solemn. "Why are you doing this?"

Without a thought, the words spill from my lips. "Because I love her. Because I've waited my entire life for her. Because when she showed up at Rush a few months ago, I realized she was no longer a little girl, so I could finally pursue her… and then she turned me down every single time I asked."

"But tonight," Auggie adds, knowing Bethany is no longer avoiding the inevitable. "I know you and I have had a difficult friendship." Dragging in a deep breath, "When Beth came to me, I initially told her no. But then I realized someone needed to protect her until you were both ready for each other. I told Beth she'd be a wife to a good man someday, and we both knew I was speaking of you. I thought it better if Beth was in my bed instead of some asshole who would mistreat her... or worse, one she'd fall in love with. I know you're pissed at me, but I did it for a good reason."

Not wanting to hear the answer, the question falls from my lips anyway, "Were you good to Bethany?"

Solemn, almost regretful– perhaps wistful –Auggie is as open and honest as I've ever seen him. "I treated Beth with respect. I gave, and she took. Not once did I have her suck me off. Everything we did was as traditional as I ever get. I only took her a handful of times in the Playroom, and it was to hammer home that she was mine and mine alone."

"I will be that for her now," I vow.

Auggie and I had been holding a conversation with his eyes closed, yet my words seem to strike him, because his green eyes flash wide open. "You don't get what you're doing, Rory. I've been Bethany's lover for the past year. I will take Rob off the menu for her if you leave well enough alone."

Fists clenched, "Do you want her that fucking much?" I snarl.

"I'm protecting you, dumbass!" Auggie shouts back at me, face turning red with the vein in his forehead bulging. "The Playroom is no place for you, and that is a compliment, Rory... and there is a reason the entrance to the Playroom is called a toll. It is the very definition of the word."

"I'll pay it," I blurt. "Beth promised to obey me for the next twenty-four hours if I gain access to the Playroom."

Green eyes slitting open, Auggie looks at me with pride and respect. "Now I understand why you are so motivated," voice thick with calculation. "You intend to marry Bethany in that timeframe, don't you?"

"Damned straight," I declare. "She's not getting away from me this time. No dating. No courting. No foreplay. Whatever you want to call it. We both know we are it for the other one– there is no sense in denying it or delaying it.

"And afterward, you won't let anyone touch your wife but you, correct?" Auggie prompts, moving the conversation in a direction I don't understand. A feral light glows from his eyes, like he's anticipating my answers before he even asks the question.

Voice dripping with possession, "Bethany will be my *wife*."

Auggie nods his head like he understands what it means to want a person all to yourself. "You'll regret this, Rory. Mark my words, you'll regret this," Auggie reaffirms his earlier claims. "However, I won't." Shoving off the door, Auggie flashes me a predatory smile. "I've waited a decade to make you respect me."

"Auggie," I grumble, feeling slightly guilty. "I can't respect you as my boss. It's impossible. I respect you as a friend and as a man, but you can't look at your equal as your boss. Isis and I work well together as a team, neither of us claiming to be in charge, both of us agreeing to let Isis take the lead. You're my friend, never my boss."

"I'm well aware of that," Auggie purrs, voice thick with anticipation. "I've tried to warn you at least a dozen times to walk away, but I realize you won't. I will not go lightly on you. I will bend you. I will force your body to betray you. I will make you crave me when you're lying awake in bed at night."

Realization dawning, Auggie's favorite activity lights up in my brain. I stumble backward, knees threatening to drop my ass to the floor. Voice breaking, "Oh, shit. You're going to make me blow you, aren't you?"

Grinning, shaking his head to and fro, Auggie growls in a voice thick with arousal, "Worse. I'm going to suck *you* off."

Sputtering, I take a dozen steps back from the man, realizing it's placing me deeper into the room, farther away from the locked exit. "How is *that* worse?" I gasp in shock. "Sucking you off would be humiliating."

"It's worse because I'll make you like it," Auggie promises arrogantly. "The show and tell in the living room was for my benefit. A nice cock gets sucked, and I just so happen to want to suck your cock very badly." Eyes fluttering shut, Auggie looks halfway to an orgasm just from the thought.

"You're sick," I gulp.

"And I have what you want." Gesturing, Auggie parts his hands, palms in the air. "I hold your future in my hands. I could fuck your future wife for the next six months, Robin too… or you could have Bethany living in your loft, playing happy homemaker by morning. Your call, Rory. I'm the only thing standing in your way."

Voice wavering with fright, "Why are you doing this?"

Auggie paces me, forcing me to draw away from him. "In truth, I'm doing this because you've never respected me. I'm doing this because I crave a thick cock as much as I do a tiny pussy. More so, I love bringing a straight man down to his knees, begging me to suck him once more, only to feel immense power when I deny him. Every single man I've sucked has asked for a repeat performance, and I've always issued a denial."

"I'll never beg," I promise.

Without arrogance, Auggie is pure confidence. "Yes, you will. And with that thick cock of yours, and if you let me touch your wife, I'd wouldn't deny you anything." Eyes salaciously drinking me in, Auggie makes me feel like a prime piece of beef. Never experiencing this level of appraisal, not with a woman, and especially not with a man, I step farther away from him, eyes looking for escape. "Hell, I might beg you for a repeat."

Scared, baffled, Auggie's aroused hunt of me across the bedroom makes me say something I should've never voiced. "Beth's right. You're fucking nuts."

"I'll be Bethany's most expensive client," Auggie says without shame. "Now take your pants off… unless you're a pussy. If so, I'll unlock the door, so you can go across town to tell Bethany to get her pretty cunt over here since we missed last night."

I pop the button on my jeans. "Rory, you are the bravest person I've ever met," Pride warring with awe, Auggie compliments me. "You deserve Bethany… now strip completely naked and sit on the chair in the corner."

My eyes flick to the chair in question. It's not a chair– it's some French or English piece of art from the nineteenth century, and Auggie wants me to sit on it while he sucks my cock. He is demented.

The only thought in my head is little Bethany as I strip down naked. I remember her when we first met, chalk all over her face and hands as we decorated the sidewalk. Then I see the incredible woman she is today, and I wonder how she felt when Auggie made her strip down naked. I think of all the times she's had to do this over the past year, and I realize I would do anything to make sure she never has to do it another single night.

"Good," Auggie purrs. "I always knew your body was male perfection," he praises, making it by far the creepiest moment of my existence, meaning I will most likely experience something far worse in a few moments. "Sit your ass at the edge of the seat with your thighs draped over the armrests."

"Why?" I breathe as I do as Auggie bid, feeling exposed and humiliated. "Never mind, I answered my own question." Limp cock resting against my belly, sac drooping down to cover my exposed asshole, I've never felt so bare in my life.

Fully clothed, Auggie kneels down between my upraised legs, and I realize why I'm in this chair. Its height is perfect for Auggie when he's kneeling on the floor– perfect for whatever he wants to do to his victim of the night.

"How many times have you made Bethany sit in this chair?" I ask stiffly.

Furry red eyebrow raised in surprise, "None. Beth and I used the bed. Rob always wanted to be more playful, but I always shut him down. In the Playroom, Beth and I always used the chaise. I told you I never treated your future wife like a whore." Auggie sounds insulted that I don't believe him.

"I wouldn't think using this chair makes a woman a whore," I mutter to myself, but then a page of Bethany's thesis flashes through my mind, and I realize Auggie *is* insane.

"Your naked ass is the first to occupy this particular seat. I've laid in bed, staring at it for hours, with the possibilities running through my mind. I always felt this chair was most versatile for play with a man."

Sucking in a deep breath, "I can't believe I'm sitting here right now, and that I'm actually going to let you do this."

"I can't either," Auggie says wryly. "I'm impressed with your nerves of steel. I bet you're freaking out on the inside."

"I wouldn't tell you if I was," I deadpan in an emotionless voice.

Smirking, "I know you wouldn't." Eyes flicking to my limp dick, Auggie scowls. "You have exactly fifteen seconds to get aroused from the time my lips touch your cock, or I will be insulted. If I'm insulted, you can get up out of this chair and go get your easy-to-arouse wife for me. Got it?"

"Shit," I hiss, freaking the fuck out. "I don't know if I can't make it hard for you, Auggie. That's asking a bit much, don't you think?"

"No, I don't," he says gravely. "I will only whore for those who want me."

"Auggie," pity thick in my voice. "You're not a whore."

Insulted by my compassion, "Shut up and make your dick hard, Rory," he demands, and then he descends.

"Christ," freaked out at the first, soft touch of Auggie's lips near my cock. Shifting on the chair, I try to get as far away from Auggie's mouth as possible. My eyes snap shut, squeezing out my reality, hoping I can play pretend to get through this surreal experience.

"Don't you fucking dare close your eyes," Auggie warns, "And if you move away from me one more time, it's game over."

I don't answer Auggie. I simply flick my eyes open and lock gazes with him. The reassuring green stare puts me at ease. *Auggie isn't going to harm me*, I repeat to myself a billion times over. He's just going to give me a blowjob. A different man would beg for the pleasure. I can get through this. It's not as if he's going to kill me.

For Bethany.

"Christ," is torn from my throat again. But this time my eyes don't snap shut and my hips don't try to retreat. It doesn't take fifteen seconds to stir to arousal either. Proving his expertise, Auggie swallows my dick and balls whole. My blunt, slightly limp dick and my entire sac are encased in the wet heat of Auggie's mouth. He groans around my cock as I grow, filling the cavern of his mouth to press down his throat. Lips wrapping tightly around me, he swallows, forcing my body to betray me. In less than five seconds, I go from flaccid to rock-hard.

Years of blowjobs have conditioned my fingers to seek hair. In order to curtail this, I grip my thighs, nails digging into my bare skin. I grit my teeth, lock my jaw, refusing to make any sounds of pleasure or distress.

I fail.

I fail miserably when Auggie rolls his gaze up to connect with mine, a look of triumph shining brightly. A small noise of panic bubbles up my throat at the sight of my cock and balls buried deep within his mouth. Kneeling between my spread thighs, head bowed down to my groin, touching me with nothing but his mouth, Auggie worships me, gives me attention like no other has before.

My girth has always made my cock look short. Every single one of the women who have sucked me off got this faraway look in their eye, like they wanted to call my dick stubby. But the truth of it is, I'm longer than average. I always joke, saying my dick is like a stout woman, almost wider than it is tall, making it look short and fat. Those same women weren't laughing when they descended on my cock, barely fitting it inside their narrow mouths.

Unlike every single time before, Auggie shows his appreciation of my girth, the shape of my cock, and the length. Never in my life have I had more than a few inches attended. Auggie doesn't suck me. He deep-throats, not only my cock, but my balls, too.

The wet slide of saliva leaves a hot trail along my taint to pool at my exposed asshole. My body tightens, every muscle glorifying in the sensation of the perfect blowjob. I begin to sweat, hot flashes of fright and pleasure warring in my body.

Auggie uses no super techniques I've had employed before. No slide of the mouth while two hands stroke my shaft. No finger sneaking to poke my ass. No twisting motion with both the hands and mouth. No tongue action. No silly teases. Auggie is all business, and I can feel his pride in his work. Auggie doesn't even bob his head. He simply uses his mouth muscles to suck me forcefully, sucking me so hard my dick will be bruised come morning. Like a well-seasoned whore, Auggie's throat grips and releases my dick in an insane rhythm of erotic torture.

Proving his word, Auggie has me hard, close to begging, and ready to pop in less than a minute into his sweet torture. I focus all of my energy into staying quiet, into refusing to writhe, into refusing to come so quickly and powerfully.

I fail.

I fail again.

I fail exquisitely.

The flick of a tongue on my asshole, while my cock and balls are still lodged deep in Auggie's mouth, shocks me into shooting my load. Sweat dripping down my brow, a primal scream torn from my throat, I surrender. I give Auggie the respect he has demanded for well over ten years. I finally realize we are not equals as my cum pours deep down his clenching throat.

By the time I'm sucked empty and dry, my fingernails have bled my thighs, and my muscles ache from tensing. Auggie pushes back from me to sit on his heels, eyes never leaving mine since this exercise in torture began.

Confused. Worried. Ashamed. Uncomfortable laughter bubbles up my throat, and I use humor to defuse my tumultuous emotions. "Can you teach Bethany how to do that with her tongue, how you sucked me off while licking at me?"

Smirking, green eyes glowing with pleasure, Auggie takes my compliment as I intended. He shakes his head to and fro. "Sorry, that's a trade secret only a guy can pull off." He points at his mouth. "Six-foot-four with a proportionate mouth. Your tiny woman cannot pull off that maneuver, and definitely not on a dick your size."

"Well, it's no wonder Rob walks around with that secret grin of his. He's thinking about how you suck his cock and rim his ass at the same time." I snort at how ridiculous I sound. I make a move to swing my legs off the armrests, causing Auggie to finally touch me with his fingertips. Just a slight pressure to my knee to still my movements.

A mask covers Auggie's face, making him appear cautious. "Rob's smiling because my mouth and hands seek him out the second we're alone. That's why."

"Ah," I breathe, understanding what Auggie is saying. No one would ever know Auggie and Rob were lovers, Isis either. In public, they do not touch, and around friends and family the contact is minimal. It makes me wonder how explosive their private reunions are. "So, am I a member of your Playroom now? Did I pass?"

Smiling brightly, "With flying colors. The first taste of a reluctant male is always the sweetest," Auggie says wryly. "Yes, you're a member of the Playroom, and you can come and go and you please. But we have one more issue to discuss."

I try to sit up again, but Auggie won't allow it. He presses his palm to my bare chest, pushing me against the backrest of the chair. His touch scalds me in to compliance.

"Bethany is under my protection, a duty I do not take lightly. The cost was sex twice a month, and there are still thirteen sessions left on her bill. It would take something major to pay that off in one lump sum."

I finally see Auggie as my boss after years of thinking it was sheer luck that he was successful in not only his illustrations, but at Rush and Revamped, too. I recognize the shrewd business side to him now.

Angry, "You aren't letting Bethany go?" I fiercely bite out, voice thick with the restraint Auggie had beat into me over the years. I thank God for that learned control, or else I'd be tearing the kneeling man limb from limb. "After what we just did?"

"You wanted to join the Playroom, and I didn't do to you anything more than I did to the other male applicants with a fine dick." Pausing, looking earnest and slightly insulted. "Well, perhaps I enjoyed it more, wanting you to enjoy it too. But I didn't give you special treatment other than showing you the depths of my oral skills. I never gave that to anybody but Rob. I figured you'd earned the respect."

Wanting to freak out and bolt out of the chair, that heavy palm keeps me in place. "You confuse the fuck out of me, Auggie. I can tell you want me to thank you or something. Your face is all intimate and open. It's creeping me out, and that's saying a lot after my dick was crammed into your piehole and you digested my spunk."

Expression soft, Auggie breathes, "I want to have sex with you."

"What?" I squawk, freaking the fuck out. My arms flail, but Auggie doesn't allow me to leave the chair. A hand presses each of my thighs to the armrests, allowing me the movement to panic but not to flee.

"Just once," he whispers while holding my gaze. He's never looked away from me since I sat in this chair of torture. "It would mean a lot to me. It would make up for your endless disrespect. It would cancel out Bethany's debt. It would make me feel like the motherfucking man... I've never had a straight guy," Auggie says slyly.

Spit flying from my mouth, "Somehow I doubt that," I snarl, furious.

"They were all curious. They wanted the Beast to fuck them. I was an oddity, like a sideshow freak." Auggie's voice is so sad that I actually begin to pity him. "But you're my friend," he manipulates me, proving that it's not just Rob who is an expert at manipulation.

"You're not in love with me, so stop looking at me like you are," I demand, thoroughly disgusted with his reverent expression.

"I care about you," Auggie whispers softly. "It would make it more fulfilling. Your reluctance would make it more thrilling. Your total surrender would make it more satisfying."

"No, fucking way, buddy," I growl. "I wasn't put on this earth to suffer your pleasure."

Intense anger and bitter disappointment wash over Auggie's features. His face turns as red as his hair. His green eyes glow with fury. "I tried to be your friend by romancing it out of you, but you forced my hand. You either let me fuck you once, or you will learn what true suffering is. Bethany owes me thirteen more fucks. I won't treat her with respect in this bed," Auggie points behind him. "I'll take Bethany like a cheap whore in the Playroom," he threatens. "I'll take that gentle, tight pussy with a vengeance, fucking her in front of you. Thirteen. Times. I'll fuck your wife in public and force you to fucking watch."

"Why are you doing this to me?" I whine, feeling betrayed by Auggie. I do the one thing I promised I'd never do. I beg him. "Don't do this. Please."

"As with the toll, this is the standard fee. I am doing nothing I wouldn't do to another member. But as my friend, I tried to do it nicely. You forced me to get nasty, Rory," Auggie bites out, looking annoyed and frustrated with me. "Your inability to respect me also forces me to get... nasty. You will do this, or I will fuck Beth, case closed. We can do this slow and sweet... or you can continue to fucking piss me off and I'll make it hurt. Your choice."

Terrified, I grit, "Can I close my eyes?"

"No," is all Auggie says as he reaches to grab something out of his back pocket.

My eyes widen with shock. "What the fuck, man? Who carries around a tube of lube and condoms in their back pocket like a deviant boy scout? Were you planning this shit?"

"Always be prepared, that's our motto." Auggie flashes me a wide grin. "Rob's a slut, so I go nowhere without these items. Men aren't exactly self-lubricating... and in a moment, you will see that lube is a helluva lot more pleasing than a spit-shine."

Shaking, shivering, trembling, and quivering: never in my life have I used those words to describe myself. I was always the big guy. The guy nobody dared to fuck with. I've never been challenged enough to be frightened. I was over-confident, so it seems.

"Just look at me, and know everything will be okay," Auggie reassures me. But the sound of his zipper lowering has my heartbeat deafening me to all other sound. "Don't look down... just look me in the eye."

Voice breaking from terror at the sound of the condom wrapper tearing open, "You're not going to prepare me first?" I try to delay the inevitable.

"No, but it won't hurt. You'll just be uncomfortable," Auggie tries to reassure me, and fails.

Eyes going wide, "Why not?" I blurt, somehow sensing the Beast is getting ready to impale my ass. My mind provides all sorts of scary imagery. Fence posts. Trains. Logs. Submarines. The Space Shuttle. All making a hole for themselves, and in my mind, that hole is my asshole.

"I am an expert at this, after all," Auggie says wryly. Instead of a laugh, Auggie groans as if in ecstasy. "But mostly, because my cock would get jealous of my fingers if they had the pleasure of breaching you first. Because you'll be tighter this way. Because regardless of how prepared you are, it's still going to be uncomfortable for you. So just relax."

I jump out of my skin at the first brush of a latex-covered dick against my sac. Shivering with trepidation, my teeth begin to chatter. "Just look me in the eye," Auggie says softly again. "I won't harm you. I promise."

Body tensing, "This is too fucking weird, man…"

"Why?" Auggie looks confused. "You're my friend. I touch you all the time. You've beaten the hell out of me for ten years, letting me return the favor. We pull no punches. It's just me touching you. Don't act like it's so invasive."

"It's your dick, Auggie… in my asshole." I shriek as Auggie starts to press inside me. "It's not like you're patting my fucking shoulder or punching me in the gut!"

Face straining, betraying his fierce control, "It's still just a part of my body, Rory. Nothing foreign. It's not like I didn't just suck your cock, and like you didn't just enjoy it…. Relax, or else I may hurt you on accident. Relax and breathe."

I breathe, but there is no relaxing. Every muscle taut in my body, I fight not to clench up and recoil from Auggie's touch. I want to close my eyes against the sight of Auggie's freckled mug, at his understanding eyes, at his parted lips. The man looks like he's in heaven, and I decide this will be the creepiest moment of my life.

Asshole burning, Auggie forces himself inside my body, one excruciating inch at a time. I grit my teeth against the pain. Discomfort? Tell that to my stretching asshole!

I reach down to hold my junk, not wanting it to come into contact with Auggie's. He intercepts my hand. "Let your balls rest on my cock. I'm fucking a man, and I want to know it. I may be bi, but as I've taught you over the years, you can't give the full force of your strength to a woman. A man is built to handle my desires." Auggie's coaxing voice charges with intense demand, "So let me feel your hairy balls rubbing at my dick."

"This is beyond disturbing," I whisper, fighting my natural urge to close my eyes. "You're insane."

Voice lulling, coaxing, drugging, Auggie chants, "Never forget this sensation. It's incomparable to anything else. The feel of a man slowly breaching your body. The way your skin beads with sweat. As if fevered, your body flashes with heat while simultaneously cooling with shivers. You don't know if you're in pain or in bliss. The intense stretch of a thick dick slicing through you, owning you. Your ass hurts, but a spot deep inside of you radiates incredible pleasure, causing the pressure in your balls to become unbearable. Your only thought is centered on your impending release."

As with the blowjob, Auggie touches me nowhere except with his cock, somehow sensing the intimate touches of a lover would freak me out. Holding my gaze, Auggie ever so slowly presses into me, stretching me to the point of searing pain, and I experience every word he uttered.

Once fully seated inside my body, Auggie's smile twists with extreme satisfaction... and then he moves. A whimper-like grunt is torn from my throat. I can feel Auggie's monster dick all the way through to my back. The pain is excruciating. The stretch is just this side of tearing... and this is Auggie being kind, gentle, slow and considerate. What damage could this man do in a fit of passion? In a fit of rage?

Teeth gritted, my body slicks with sweat. I have no term for the sensation of Auggie invading my body. Pain? Discomfort? Agony? It's as emotional as physical. I doubt in my lifetime I'll ever sort out how I feel in this moment. Auggie forces me to respect him, to see him as the controlling, demanding, powerful, caring and giving man that he is.

Fully-clothed while I am buck-assed naked, Auggie barely swivels his hips, finding a twisting motion that satisfies his cravings without bleeding me. "Breathe, Rory... trust me... and open up your eyes again."

"Shit," I hiss, not even realizing my body took control of my mind. I'd subconsciously closed my eyes, blocking out my surreal reality. Betraying me in another way, my body arouses beneath Auggie's expert thrust. As promised, I feel ill through the experience but my dick is engorged and my balls are high and tight– so tight to my body that Auggie's cock no longer caresses them on every thrust of his hips.

I ache.

Bruising, fingernails grip my thighs until crescents indent my flesh, pooled with blood. My teeth are gritted, jaw locked against the indescribable sensation. My toes are curled, trying to gain me the leverage they give me walking through life. My eyes are locked with Auggie's, refusing to glance anywhere else, fearing witness to my shame. I don't want to know what I look like while being fucked, imprinted in my memories for a lifetime of remembrance.

I can't believe a man is fucking me. No, not fucking. Auggie is having sex with me. I fear a thorough fucking would murder me in all the ways that count.

Shame changing to curiosity. Whimpers of bitter pain turning to grunts of agony-fueled pleasure. I succumb to Auggie's onslaught. Noticing the change in me, the tide forces Auggie to climax. Utterly silent, stare intense and unrelenting, Auggie rolls me under and takes me down with him.

In deafening silence, no grunts, no groans, no moans, we get off at the same fucking time. Auggie flexing and jerking inside me, filling the condom, with me splattering my chest with my scalding release. In an intense battle-of-wills that rivals any fought in our lifetime, we prove who has the most stringent control… and it's a dead-heat.

A tie.

Auggie is no boss of mine. We are equals. He may have entered my body, but he didn't fuck me. Refusing to blink as he reads my thoughts, Auggie nods his head in acceptance.

Slowly pulling from my body, exhausted, emotionally distraught, Auggie looks just as I feel. Sheepishly, Auggie tucks himself into his pants, avoiding my gaze now that the deed is done. With a deep sigh, he rises to his feet in one fluid motion. Still, without looking at me, Auggie kisses my forehead.

Speaking against my flesh, "I'm proud of you, kid. You did good." Pulling away, still refusing to look at me,

"Congratulations. You and Bethany deserve each other, and you'll be very happy. Name your first born after me, will ya?" He releases a laugh, but it's strained.

Heading toward the door, I stop Auggie in his tracks. "Don't make me prove my trust to you again, old friend. Got it?"

"Understood," Auggie whispers as he unlocks the door with the skeleton key. "Our trust is resolute after this, Rory. Resolute," Auggie promises as he leaves me alone.

I sit for an indeterminate amount of time, mind reeling, and I realize I could sit here forever and never come to terms with what just happened. Slowly rising to my feet in a stew of contradiction, I decide it's time to move forward, toward Bethany.

Ashamed.

Proud.

Scared.

Courageous.

Enlivened.

Feeling like a whore.

Feeling like a God among men.

I want to take a scalding shower and wash away the evidence of the events from the last hour. But at the same time, I want to wear my drying spunk as a badge of honor.

Both Robin and Auggie were wrong. I did this for Bethany. Therefore, I will never regret it.

CHAPTER EIGHT

Bethany Oman

Augustus Kline: Reigning supreme within a deviant kingdom of his own creation, by Bethany Oman. Pg. 279

Auggie has a fascination with the fragility of females. One would think sex with a man with a great wealth of experience would be anything but mediocre. A Playroom, an unending stream of conquests, two lifelong lovers, and Augustus Kline was obsessed with normalcy. Sex with a 'wife' was in a bed, with the female on her back or in Auggie's lap. Sex with a 'whore' only involved Auggie's oral pleasure. Contradictorily, Auggie refused such attentions from his 'wifely' partners. There is a definite divide within Augustus Kline's mind when it comes to the fairer sex.

Eyes darting to the clock for the billionth time, I've used the past four hours since Rory left to work on my thesis. By hour two, I assumed Rory's mission was a failure, and I had no reason to worry about whatever harebrained scheme Rory dreamed up for my twenty-four hours of obedience. I was worried for a few hours, since I remember how devious Rory was as a child. He had a wicked imagination, and he'd tell me stories for hours. I feared those stories would manifest into whatever he had planned for my servitude.

Slumped over, resting on my elbows, I stare at the cursor blinking on my laptop screen. I've tried to keep myself out of my thesis. There is an experience that must be documented, but to do so exposes the lengths I went to achieve my goals.

I want to type out the night Auggie lost all control and fucked me like a whore. It was an unforgettable experience that left me feeling like a real woman, not the whore Auggie thought it would make me. There are three speeds to Auggie: slow and steady (boring), emotionally distraught thrusting (words of adoration directed at Isis while sobbing), and the unbridled, brutality of a thorough fucking by the Beast (unforgettable).

No sex with Auggie is forgettable, not with that cock or the emotional toll, but it saddens me that he refuses to unleash the best part of him because he is afraid of harming his partner. Even when Rob joined us in bed, Auggie treated him like fragile glass.

After a year of witnessing every hedonistic activity imaginable, straight sex in a bed without any emotional connection doesn't do a thing for me. I want passion. I want lust. I hunger to experience more... and I only felt it briefly when Auggie released his inner beast, and it still wasn't enough for me.

What to do... what to do?

Do I add that experience, knowing it shows just how wounded Auggie truly is? But if I do, I will have to place myself in the position to be called out on my own sexual deviancy. Who fucks their thesis subject?

"Not dressed, I see," comes from behind me, startling the shit out of me again.

"Jesus, Rory," I sputter. "One of these times I'm going to be wearing pants, and I'll finally wet them. Seems like your huge feet would make some noise when you walk." First, I save my work, and then I shut my laptop down. I spin around in my chair, scared to learn my fate.

Arms crossed over his wide chest, Rory leans against my front door, a knowing glint in his eye. "Just think," he begins, uncrossing his arms, "If you'd actually lock your door, I'd have to knock first."

"Ah," I breathe, unable to argue against his well-made point. "You've got me there. I take it you didn't get into the Playroom," I say confidently.

Breaking away from the door, Rory stalks across my tiny apartment, looking every bit a predator. "You take it wrong," he states, stunning me. "You are looking at the newest member of the Playroom." Proud, preening, Rory doesn't look like a man who was manipulated by Auggie. Knowing they are friends, I wonder if Auggie gave Rory a pass.

Suspicious, "Did you make me wait all that time so I'd think I was scot-free?"

Taken aback, Rory startles. "No," he says slowly. "My *toll* took some time, and then I had arrangements to make for the twenty hours left on our agreement. I've been busy." Blue eyes narrowing, "Will you be honoring your bet, or will you be reneging?"

Patiently waiting, I can tell Rory will *make* me honor our bet, or else. "Honoring," I state through clenched teeth. Hello Kitty nightshirt be damned, I think I'm going to wet myself. "I trust you," *sort of.* "What was your toll?"

Face twisting into a grimace, Rory shudders. "Later," he ends that uncomfortable subject. "Our first date is almost eighteen years in the making, so I wanted to make it special. I want to see you in your nicest dress, and it doesn't have to be… too hot. Then I need you to pack an overnight bag."

"What?" I breathe, confused. "Where are we going?"

A feral smile twisting his lips, Rory purrs, "Vegas, baby. I'm taking your sweet behind to Las Vegas."

Abruptly standing from my desk chair. "Rory Essex, have you lost your goddamned mind? I'm eating Ramen from my parents' cupboards and living above a shed. I can't even pay this month's cellphone bill. I can't afford a plane ticket or gambling."

Pointing at his chest, Rory growls deeply from his chest, "I earned your obedience. Our first date, our first time, and the first night of the rest of our lives together begins right now. I've earned the right to take *my* Bethany to Vegas," he snarls, looking animalistic. "No gambling. I want to treat you like a queen: decadent food, exciting shows, and an impressive hotel room where we fuck each other into a coma. Hopefully, you will allow me to extend our twenty-four hours into several days, with the obedience ending twenty hours from now. Let me do this for *us*," he begs, eyes bleeding hunger.

Excited, wanting to go, but the grownup in me rears her wise head. "What about work? What about the landlord I'm supposed to meet in the morning with Essie? I have responsibilities, Rory."

"I'll call your boss while you get around." Rory gives me a look that screams guilt.

Stalking toward him, "What are you up to, mister?" I eyeball Rory, trying to read his thoughts. "You're up to something I may not like."

Eyes glowing with happiness, or madness, Rory smiles at me, and he is absolutely breathtaking. "You may not like it, but you'll do it," he warns, voice getting deeper by the second. "And I can guarantee, you *will* enjoy it."

Scoffing, I just stare at Rory, scared shitless over what's to come. Voice breaking, suspicions rising, heart beating out of my chest, "Why Vegas? I know why I'd be taking your ass to Vegas…" I trail off, shivering.

"Get dressed. Pack a bag. Lock this place down." Rory turns away from me, giving me as much privacy as my tiny apartment will allow. He pulls his cellphone from his back pocket, drawing my eyes to the perfect lines of his firm behind. I sigh, I can't help myself. I'd do anything for this man.

Looking over his shoulder, amusement glowing from his eyes, "Hurry along, now. We don't want to miss our flight." I shake my head like a dumbass, speechless. "Oh, and Bethany?"

"Yeah," I mutter, voice thick, mouth dry.

Rory's lust-filled gaze tracks over my body, returning the look I gave his ass. "Don't wear any panties underneath that dress."

CHAPTER NINE

When pigs fly, they go wee... wee... wee, all the way to Las Vegas

Wiggling my butt into the buttery-soft leather seat, I unhook my seatbelt just after takeoff. "Wow, Rory," I utter in amazement. "If this is any indication on what dating you will be like, I'm fucking scared. First class? Did you win the lottery? Do you secretly have a trust fund from a wealthy ancient uncle I didn't know about? Are you a drug dealer?"

All Rory does is smirk in reply. Turning in his seat so we have the intimacy of face-to-face, "And I even gave you the window seat. I'm such a catch," he says sarcastically, but I can hear the underlying pride in his tone.

Getting serious, realistic, I breathe, "Can you afford this? Really? I'm not complaining, because Lord knows my parents couldn't ever afford to treat us like this. So it's like..." I whisper in awe, "Wow... I don't want to offend your pride or anything, but can you afford this? I don't want you to think I have to be wooed with money."

Turning equally serious, Rory leans into me, brushing my hair away from my face. Pressing his lips to the shell of my ear, he whispers, "Most families save a lifetime for this trip. I want it to be special."

"Huh?" I grunt, confused. *This trip?*

Rory places a gentle kiss to my throat, causing me to shiver with anticipation. My body breaks out in a sweat just from the subtle contact. Pulling away, he speaks. "Beth, Auggie bought Rush when I was a senior. I've had a fulltime job for eight years straight. I have no student loans to pay back, no credit card debt, no rent or a mortgage or even utilities, and my commute to work takes me a heartbeat. I can afford to pamper you for a few days every once in a while, just as long as we don't make a habit out of it."

"Isis pays that well, huh?" Shaking my head to and fro, I feel like an idiot. "I thought I was being crafty, being responsible, for taking less than a year to get my cosmetology license. I saw all the townies struggling, and I'd make fun of them. But here you are, no higher education, and you're better off because of it. I'm strapped down with debt up to my ears until I turn sixty fucking years old.

Looking sympathetic, "Well, not all of us have a job land into their laps. I'm very lucky," he breathes, emotions written across his face. "But most of us aren't fit to make a real difference in someone's life. Bethany, that's a real accomplishment, debt be damned."

"I don't know about what effect I'll have on my future patients' lives. I could suck at counseling," I correct. "Yeah," blushing profusely, so happy someone acknowledges all my hard work, "I didn't have it in me to go the extra mile and become a true doctor of psychiatry. There is a big difference between a psychiatrist and a psychologist. Starting in December, I'll be interning for the next two years to gain my license. I just didn't have it in me to go the medicine route."

Smiling like he finds me foolish for feeling inadequate, "Apples and oranges, Beth. You need to be proud of yourself. You're doing something you were meant to do, helping people who truly need your help. I'm proud of you," Rory says, getting choked up, which in turns draws tears to my eyes.

Palm flying out in a soft swat to his chest, "Oh, stop." I look away, gazing out the window to the blue-gray night sky. I marvel at the difference of flying in the middle of the night instead of in the early morning hours. I've only been on a plane three other times, all flying to Georgia to visit my grandparents. But this feels different. Late at night, the tranquility of first class mixed with the silence of sleeping passengers, and being with Rory instead of my parents. It's surreal.

"Wow," I breathe against the window, a silly smile twisting my lips. "Wow."

"Would you like a blanket?" the flight attendant asks, leaning down over the seat in front of us. "Can I get you anything else?"

"A blanket would be great, please." Rory smiles sweetly as he accepts the gray blanket. "Thanks," he says in dismissal.

Turning to me, "Let's rest a bit. It's going to be a mile a minute once we land."

"What are you up to?" I ask of the ecstatic light glowing from Rory's eyes.

Sliding his arm around my shoulders, Rory hunkers down. He draws the blanket over both of our laps. "Not a thing, darlin'. I'm just cuddling with my lil pup."

"Rory," I sigh out. "I don't like that nickname."

Cheek brushing my hair, voice laced with confusion, "Why?"

"I'm not proud of the lengths I've gone to write my thesis, Rory." I admit a hard truth that has been plaguing me. "I haven't done anything I'm truly ashamed of yet, but I could have. So when you call me lil pup, it draws attention to what I could've become, what I still could become."

Softly chuckling in my ear, Rory tugs me closer, nearly drawing me into his lap. "Bethany," he laughs out my name. "I'm not calling you lil pup because of your Playroom theatrics. Since you were a little shit with pigtails, you've been following me around like a puppy wagging its tail. Waiting for me to get home from school, peering out your front window. Waiting on your lawn for me to come home to visit my parents."

"Huh?" I mutter when Rory stops talking.

"Um... it's slightly derogatory. I just realized this now. You're gonna kick my ass if I tell you the truth."

Muscles clenching, I turn frigid in Rory's embrace. "Spit it out," I demand, worried about why he'd call me lil pup.

Hesitant, "Okay. Okay... when you were a kid, your antics reminded me of a puppy eagerly waiting for its master. My dog, Rufus, wasn't as excited to see me as you were. That's why... not now, like when you were five years old," Rory stammers, causing me to laugh.

Giggling into my palm, "Derogatory in the extreme, but you're oh so right!" Blushing fiercely. "I'm so embarrassed. I made a fool out of myself every single time I saw you. I'd do the dumbest shit to gain your attention, but then I was thankful you didn't notice. If I ever have a daughter, I'm locking her in her bedroom."

Nuzzling my hair with the tip of his nose, Rory makes a pleasing sound in the back of his throat. "I loved it. I noticed even when I was pretending not to notice." Voice threaded with affection, "It made me feel special. You were precious to me, more so now than ever."

Pulling the blanket higher, until it reaches our shoulders, Rory completely engulfs me with his body. His arms are wrapped around me, his thighs are clenching around one of mine. His hands are rubbing whatever they can gain access to. Rory rumbles a happy sound, so content to sit like this forever.

Since I'm a girl, and we say stupid shit when uncomfortable, usually shit that ruins the mood to make us feel less uncomfortable. As a trained psychologist, I recognize this. But as a woman, I can't stop myself from doing it anyway. It's the hormones, I think.

"What was your toll?"

Barking out a sharp laugh, Rory looks around the cabin to make sure he didn't wake any of the other passengers. He receives a grin from the cute flight attendant instead of a reprimand, and I don't like that one bit.

Laughter infusing his voice, Rory whispers wryly, "I was told it was the standard toll for those with a '*fine*' dick."

Knowing Auggie's practices, I'm not surprised. But I am shocked that Rory went through with it. "Are you okay? Did Auggie enjoy it? Did you enjoy it?" I enter interrogator-mode, wanting all the juicy details to analyze for later.

Being the last conscious beings on the flight, the attendant had turned the lights down lower when we cuddled up underneath the blanket. In the dark of the cabin, I can't tell if Rory is embarrassed, but his body temperature rises, indicating he's wearing one helluva blush.

"Auggie's fucked in the head," Rory says instead of answering. "From that page in your thesis and the odd shit he was spewing, he needs some help. It's no wonder Isis is always in a foul mood... but, he's probably pretty fucking happy right now. Even though, Auggie did seem out of it when he left me."

"Tell me about it," I grumble. "Auggie's missionary bullshit got old fast. The only time I really, really enjoyed myself was when he lost his control and fucked me hard." I admit, and then I realize I should've probably kept my motherfucking mouth shut. No guy wants to hear about the previous guy's prowess in bed.

"Oh, really?" Rory draws, sounding amused yet annoyed. His fingertips walk down my belly, scrunching up my sundress, and sneak between my thighs. I squeak, eyes darting around to see if anyone noticed. "Shh... calm down," Rory breathes into my ear. When I relax, "That's a good lil pup."

"Moving a bit fast for a first date, aren't ya, Rory?" I try to chastise him but it comes out breathy and thready. "Haven't even had our first real kiss yet, and you're already going for the puss."

Fingers wiggling in between my lips, Rory slips against my private flesh, feeling the proof of how aroused he makes me. A pleased sound thrums in Rory's chest at the feel of how wet I am for him. "Oh, I have something special planned for our first real kiss," Rory murmurs near my ear, causing me to shiver from the intensity of his words. "Now, as for Auggie, he lied to me, saying he never fucked you."

"It was just the one time," I quickly stammer, quivering from the content of our conversation and Rory's sneaky fingertips. "Rob pushed him to it... Hey, you never answered my questions," I remind Rory, hoping he will stop his ministrations... hoping he will never stop.

Palm cupping the back of my knee, Rory draws my leg up, hooking my thigh over top of his own, fully opening me to his touch. I gaze down, making sure it's not obvious what is going down between us underneath the blanket. "I'll answer when you give me details," Rory murmurs, sounding lust-drunk.

"Ah," I purr. "I get why you requested no panties." Rory laughs, and I shamelessly join him. Blushing, I tell the story of the only time I'd been fucked. "It was maybe a month or two ago. It wasn't... it wasn't until after Willow smartened up and got away from Mr. Kline that Auggie had Rob join us. Auggie was making amends to Rob, I think."

"No shit," Rory grunts, sounding furious. "I wanted to gut Auggie when he touched that little girl."

"Not so little," I defend. "Willow is a grown woman with grown woman needs. I understand how she feels. With that being said, Auggie needs his ass kicked," I emphatically agree.

"I'm sure Rob mentally kicked Auggie's ass," Rory mutters, lost in thought.

I want Rory with me in the moment, so I say outrageous things, but they are all the truth. "It was tame shit between the three of us. Auggie taking me missionary-style with Rob watching, Rob begging to join, Rob pleading to do something fun. They never touched– ever. Rob, sick of it, took an opportunity to really piss Auggie off."

"It's his life's work," Rory sounds impressed at the lengths Rob will go to push Auggie to the brink.

"Auggie was running late, and Rob got that evil twinkle in his eye. You know the one," I say in utter amusement."

Rory snorts, and then says, "I know the look. Rob's been wearing it since the day I met him. Scares the living daylights outta me, it does."

"Evil grin mixed with my peach schnapps' buzz... so when Auggie walked in, he found Rob banging away at me from behind." Mouth dry, my voice is thick. A shudder rolls up my spine from the memory, but it's Rory's expert touch that makes it radiate all throughout my body. I turn my face against Rory's shoulder when his fingers picks up speed on my well-stroked cunny. Proving my need to analyze the deviant mind, both Rory and I are enjoying my tale. Most men would have been furious to hear of *their* woman's exploits. Hearing and seeing are two different things, though.

"Slow up," I warn when my body starts to enjoy Rory's fingertips way too much. Panting against his shoulder, fingers curling into his forearms, thighs quivering in delight, I'm on the cusp of coming. "Shit," I hiss. "I've waited an eternity for you to touch me like this. It's even stranger that you're doing it while I'm telling you about doing two other guys."

"That was the past," Rory grunts roughly. A finger disappears into the depths of my body, going knuckle-deep before twisting like a corkscrew of ecstasy. "My fingers are proof that you're with me. I've waited even longer to touch you, Bethany. I need to hear this. But I need to touch you to reassure myself."

"Should I stop?" I half-cry, because Rory isn't messing around. He is going to bring me to climax on this motherfucking plane. My body beads with sweat. My thighs quiver so violently that my muscles ache. My pussy contracts, sucking Rory's digit in deeper, keeping it within me always.

"Keep going," Rory breathes roughly, nearly gasping into my ear. His lips brush against me with every word he speaks. "I wanna hear it."

"God, it was *soooo* good," I moan out. Even to my own ears, I'm not sure if I'm speaking of the past or what's going on right this instant. "I'd never been fucked before. Not sex–*fucked*. Raw. Rough. Real. I've had one-night-stands with fumbling coeds, and then Auggie and his bed-sex. But Rob, he knew what he was doing, and I was really getting into it when Auggie tore him off me, shouting about whores." I chuckle. It's not funny that Auggie is demented. But at the same time, it is humorous after the fact. "Losing his shit, Auggie cursed up a storm while he fucked me from behind. Hard. And it was glorious," I murmur in a dreamy lust-filled voice. "I needed it."

Whimpering in my ear, Rory's fingers find a punishing rhythm while his other hand cups my breast, and then squeezes roughly. A moan is torn from my throat, one I smother in the fabric of Rory's shirt.

"Afterward, I basically passed out, blissed out of my mind. Half-awake, Auggie went crazy on Rob, doing to him what he did to me. Rob was crying, blubbering about how it had been too long. My eyes were hazy, so I didn't really see. But when I woke up hours later, ready to leave, Rob was on top of Auggie, and Auggie was crying. Auggie kept telling Rob not to treat him kindly, and Rob said he needed it. Rob was saying how Auggie needed to fuck us like whores, and then be made love to by him. It was surreal. The guy is wacked in the head."

Fingers slowing, voice introspective, "Auggie called himself a whore tonight. He's got some deep-seated issues, for sure. He said he gave me the type of blowjob he'd only give to Rob."

Body jolting from the imagery Rory's words placed in my mind, gentle touch or not, I'm ready to explode. "I can't believe you let him suck you off," I gasp, straining not to cum.

Chuckling breathlessly, Rory's touch turns violent, exquisite, exactly what I need. Two fingers plunging into me deeply with his thumb rubbing perfect circles around my clit. Thank goodness, the blanket dampens the sound of my wet flesh sucking at Rory's fingers.

"Ohhhh…" I pant, quivering. "Don't let me make too much noise. I can't believe I'm gonna come for Rory fucking Essex!"

Palm leaving my breast to cup my mouth, Rory murmurs in utter disbelief, "I can't believe I let Augustus Kline fuck me…"

All the energy in the universe collides, collects, and then implodes in my womb. A silent scream is torn from my throat, and any and all sound that does expel is dampened by Rory's palm. I lock my body, muscles clamped down to halt my need to writhe. The only movement I allow is my pussy milking at Rory's thick fingers.

"Fuck," Rory breathes against my cheek. "That was the most beautiful sight I've ever seen. I'm never letting you go, Bethany," Rory warns, but it sounds like a promise. A promise I'd gladly make him keep.

Body tapped of energy, I fall lax. I pass out in Rory Essex's arms with a huge, silly smile on my face and *Lil Pup* echoing in my ears.

CHAPTER TEN

Eyes closed, I rest my head against the leather car seat– another luxury Rory said we couldn't live without. I quickly figured out where the man's loyalties lie. All the while Rory was making fun of my extensive Blu-ray collection, he's been wasting money on horsepower, leather, and chrome. The guy has a serious car fetish.

Half-asleep as we drive to the hotel from the airport, my words are jumbled together. "I can't believe you rented a car exactly like the one you have at home."

The manly man erupts from Rory's throat. "It's not a car. It's a Dodge Challenger. Don't insult my baby."

I snicker, but Rory's animalistic warning growl informs me he's being deadly serious. I so badly want to say, "*It's just a car.*" But he would likely kick my behind. "Well, do you feel like you're cheating on your baby?" I tease.

"No," Rory grumbles. I pop an eyelid to take a quick look at him. Rory is pouting while stroking the steering wheel with obvious affection. "I got the same color so it's like I'm driving the same *machine*. Mustn't upset either of my Phantom Black ladies."

"Oh, Lord," I groan. "My Toyota is an *it*. Not a she, a baby, or a lady. *It's* a car, not a *machine*."

Huffing a laugh, Rory turns his head slightly to the side so he can glance at me. "Because it's a Toyota. A Corolla is *not* a Challenger."

"Men," I sigh out. "I'm taking a nap."

I swear Rory whispers underneath his breath, "*You need a machine purring under your ass.*"

The *car* draws to a stop, jarring me to complete alertness. At seven-something in the morning, I expected to go check into the hotel and have a quick nap, as in five or six hours of uninterrupted sleep in a row. I gaze around at the one-story cheap-looking buildings surrounding us. I'm confused as to why we aren't on the Vegas Strip, with all the huge casinos.

"Are we lost?" I ask Rory because he's staring at his cellphone's GPS with great concentration. "I mean, how hard is it to locate Las Vegas?" I snort, roll my eyes, and think a lot of uncomplimentary thoughts about the male sex in general. I remember my father always refusing to stop and ask for directions, refusing to trust my mom or me when we held the map. But with the advent of GPS, guys have even bigger egos on navigation.

Setting his cellphone on the dashboard, Rory turns to me, expression suddenly serious. He reaches out to take my hand, looking at me like he's about to tell me my dog died. That's what this reminds me of– the same expression was on Rory's face when he told me Rufus went away to the big farm in the sky.

Swallowing, licking his lips, face solemn– almost scared – Rory makes my heart slow, and then beat into hyper-drive. Giving my hand a gentle squeeze, his words do *not* reassure me. "You are a woman of her word. I need you to trust me. I need you to do this. I need you to not hold this shitty union over my head for the rest of my life. Please," he begs.

"What?" I squeak out. My hand pulls from Rory's to immediately unhook my seatbelt. "What's going on?" I half-shriek as my eyes dart around to the surrounding buildings. "Why aren't we at the Bellagio? What's going on?"

Blue eyes pinning me, Rory has never looked so stark in all of his life. "I have ten hours left on our deal. You promised to do anything I say, without question. Do you trust me?"

Panting wildly, "I used to–" gulp "–until now."

"I understand why you feel that way. I'm being very cloak and dagger," he says while wearing a weak grin.

"No shit," I blurt out. "Get to why we're sitting outside of…" I turn to look out the window once more, eyes lighting on a pink and black disaster of a wedding chapel. I gulp, "Wildly Wedded Wife?"

Shrugging, not looking repentant at all, "I can't do this the traditional way. I'm a man who knows what he wants, has waited nearly twenty years for her to grow up, has spent another seven months trying to convince her to go out with him, and now he has her in his clutches." Grabbing for my hand, Rory grasps my wrist in a tight grip. "I'm not letting you go until you're tied to me irrevocably," he warns.

Eyes bulging from my skull, I'm rendered speechless– a first for me. Panting breathlessly, chest rushing up and down, muscles quivering, my body knows what's going down, even if my mind has yet to get with the program.

Pleading with me, "You want this just as much as I do. Our absence would be a year or two, and when we'd see each other next, it was as if it were yesterday. That's how it's always been for us. We'd just pick up our conversation where we left off. We were best friends the instant we met. But more so, we wanted each other in a way that was not platonic. Electric. Explosive." Tilting his head to the side, intense hunger washes over Rory's features. "Erotic," is a rumbling purr from his chest.

"Shit," I hiss, body shivering. I shake so hard, my muscles ache from trying to still the movement. Toes jittering in my sandals, palms sweating against Rory's hands, thighs quivering, stomach bubbling, heart exploding, face burning, mind whirling, I turn into a ball of energy that cannot remain sedentary.

"I could get down on bended knee," rolls off Rory's tongue as he pulls something from his pocket. "But we're past that. I could give you a huge wedding, but you're too frugal to enjoy it. I could actually ask you to marry me, but you're too logical to say yes right away. I can't take the risk that you'd say no if you had the chance to over-think us."

"Jesus," I mutter in awe, amazed that someone on this planet actually '*gets*' me.

An excited light blazes from Rory's blue eyes. That potent look of victory renders me motionless, thoughtless– speechless. "I'm not going to ask. I'm not going to let you think." Grasping my hand, Rory slides a shiny, glittering ring on my finger. "The engagement ring my Grandfather Essex gave to his wife, my grandmother, before they were married," he whispers reverently. Plucking something else from his pocket while smiling wryly, "Also the world's shortest engagement, seeing as how Grandma was pregnant with my uncle at the time. These," he shows me two gold bands, "Were my grandparents' wedding rings… and we'll be using them in about ten minutes."

"But… but…" I stammer out. "Your grandparents are still alive."

Snorting, "Married life was agreeable for them– they went from skinny to happy-fat. Grandma took the set of rings off ages ago, said it was cutting her circulation off." Smiling as if reliving a pleasant memory. "Grandpa said he wasn't gonna wear girly jewelry if she wasn't gonna, and took his ring off too."

Laughing, freaking the fuck out, "What the… how'd you get them?"

"I was standing right there while they were bickering. I was maybe ten years old or so. Grandpa called Grandma an old, fat harpy, and then pressed the rings into my hand. He told me to give 'em to a girl I'd make so happy she'd get fat, and then he swatted my grandmother on the ass as he left the room. Grandma was beaming with pride when I ran outta the house like my feet were on fire."

Mystified, I mumble, "And you kept them?"

"Because I knew who I was going to give them to someday." Rory smiles at me while reaching up to chuck me under the chin. "C'mon, time to make my grandparents proud. I gotta bride to make fat and happy, and she has no say in it whatsoever– she promised to obey." Looking at his cellphone, "But only for the next few hours. Don't you dare say the obey bullshit if they pull that out in the vows. I want you bickering with me, keeping me on my toes."

Without thought, my body is ejected from the car, propelled by a lifetime of chasing after Rory Essex. My brain wants to analyze all the angles, weigh all the options, and determine if this fits into my life plan. But the little girl in me is ecstatic, thriving on the urge to fly by the seat of her pants, to just let go and follow her emotions. Around the time I knew I would never catch up to Rory, always being years left behind, I lost my spontaneity.

Until now, I never realized Rory was the one who made me feel free to be me. There are no expectations to live up to, no goals to achieve, and no pressure. Rory would just be happy being by my side, in anything we do… and the little girl in me remembers how intoxicating, how happy, how comforting and loving the sensation of Rory's presence can be. I want to bathe in that warm feeling for the rest of my life, facing everything head-on as long as Rory is at my side.

I make it halfway up the sidewalk to the front of Wildly Wedded Wife before Rory can catch up with me. His relieved laughter mingles with my insane giggle. "Hold up!" Rory pulls me to a stop. "Here," he yanks something out of his pocket– fabric. "Put this on."

"What the hell?" I giggle when my mind finally reasons out that the swath of tulle is a mini-veil. After some awkward adjustments, many laughs, and plenty of eye rolling, "How do I look?"

"Like *my* bride," Rory says, voice infused with pride. "Now, do you understand why I wanted you to wear a nice dress, one that wasn't too hot?"

"Oh. My. God." Chuckles spill from my throat. "I thought you meant hot because we were going to hotter than blazes Nevada, not hot as in slutty. I wore a sundress, and for the rest of my days this thing is going to be my wedding dress. W-O-W!" I would have picked out something nicer, more bride-like, and taken a nap, and brushed my hair. I looked like hell warmed over.

"I brought this for pictures," Rory teases me, wiggling his cellphone in front of my face. "Gotta immortalize you in this cheesy headgear. C'mon, let's elope."

Being towed to the door, "That's why you said this was the trip families save up for lifetimes to afford. That's why the first class airfare and the expensive hotel. That's why you wouldn't kiss me properly. Isn't it? Whoa…" I'm rendered speechless again.

I'm standing in a Las Vegas chapel named Wildly Wedded Wife, and the name fits the place to a T. Loud 1980s décor. Wall-to-wall pink carpeting with gray paint-speckled walls. A high-glossed white arbor with fake silk flowers twisting around the rungs– dusty, faded roses and ivy. Mendelssohn's Wedding March is blaring from the speakers in its staticy glory.

"I made an appointment," Rory is rumbling to someone, but hell if I know who since my eyes are glued to the tacky awesomeness surrounding me. "Essex at eight a.m."

"Oh!" I grunt, getting impatient. "Oh, Rory?" I tug on his hand. "Oh. Hey?" I tug harder until his ear is within whispering distance. Eyes bugging out of my skull in wonderment, "Is that woman… the woman over there by the plastic wedding cake… is she a… tranny?"

"What?" Rory snorts, looking at me like I'm the cutest thing he's ever seen. "Probably. Why?"

"Can I interview her?" I beg, voice dripping with excitement. "Can I?"

Blue eyes heavily hooded, Rory just looks at me, refusing to answer. He leans down and kisses the tip of my nose. "Maybe we can come back tomorrow. Today is about us."

Feeling deflated, but not because I can't interview the woman with the magenta foil wig, bulging spandex hot pants, black thigh-high boots, and a penis. I feel badly that the environs enthralled me to the point that I forgot why I was here.

Bethany Oman is no more, as pronounced by an Asian Elvis impersonator.

Standing beneath the cheesy arbor covered in dusty, faded flowers, Rory and I repeat our vows to one another. But hell if I know what I said, since I was so lost in Rory's eyes, the elated cadence of his voice, and the warmth of his hand as he slipped his grandmother's ring onto my finger– it fit perfectly, and I'll be sure to get as big as my mom so I can pass the rings on to my children and grandchildren.

Our future is sealed by a man with fuzz glued to his face as sideburns and a heavily accented voice. "I pronounce you Mr. and Mrs. Rory Essex. You may kiss your bride."

Eighteen years ago, I ran headlong out my front door and stumbled into the boy of my dreams. Years rolled by as my little girl crush forced me to steal a press of a kiss from a boy who was trying to keep me at arm's length. Rory grew into a man, and waited for me to grow into a woman. Now we are sealed as man and wife– no chasing, no catching up, no slowing down, or going backward. Our lives finally balanced when they were supposed to intersect– connect.

Confident, my name is Bethany Essex, because I know Rory is the man for me. Making the first move, as always, I grab the front of Rory's shirt, fisting it in my fingertips to yank him down to my lips. "You're not getting away from me this time," I warn against his lips. "You're mine now, mister."

Laughing, elated, face bright, and eyes shiny, Rory just smiles against my lips, no doubt reliving the memory of pushing me down three steps to land on my ass, and how I did the same to him only a few days ago.

In the blink of an eye, we are fused to one another. Mouths, lips, tongues dueling. Fingers twisted in each other's hair. Bodies trying to meld into one another. Moaning, nearly crying in ecstasy, I lose myself to my husband.

Playroom rules apply in Las Vegas, as the tranny and Elvis whoop and holler in appreciation of our show. The parishioners of every church in Fairport would have been screaming damnation and Hellfire at our lust-fueled display, but our new friends appreciate our hedonism.

Slowly pulling away, Rory's lips are cherry-red, his eyes are heavily hooded, and his face is flushed. We breathe at the same time, "Hurry."

CHAPTER ELEVEN

Lips fused to a whisker-stubbled neck. Tongue rasping against the grain of Rory's short beard. Teeth sinking into the most delectable flesh I've ever tasted. Hands roughly wrenching Rory's t-shirt from where it's caught in his seatbelt. Breath shallow and husky as I pant with wild abandon. *Hurry* echoes in my ears almost as loudly as Rory's tortured protests to slow down.

"Hurry," I breathe against Rory's damp throat– skin wet from my tongue. "Park the fucking car before I'm forced to tear your fly open and sit on your dick while you drive."

Hand violently gripping the gearshift, hips jerking off the seat, foot pressing on the accelerator, reeving the engine because the car is now in park, Rory turns feral. "I don't know how the hell we got to the hotel and remained alive. You nearly killed us several times over. You gave that guy at the stoplight quite the show… I think I just came in my pants."

Insanely curious, my exploring fingertips abandon Rory's t-shirt to the seatbelt and conquer his pants instead. Palm cupping his impressive bulge, "You didn't come yet," I purr in a lust-fueled voice. "But you will be."

Lunging out of the *machine* like his ass is on fire, Rory is getting our luggage before I even have a chance to get my seatbelt off. He's either eager to get me alone, or eager to get away from my roaming mouth and hands.

Crawling from the car, I stand on wobbly legs. I whimper as a rivulet of moisture glides down my inner thigh. I curse Rory for asking me to go without panties as much as I praise him for the inspired suggestion.

The next few minutes go by in a haze, a haze where I concentrate on the stickiness coating my thighs and the insanity raging in my womb. Paranoid, I fear people can see *and* smell my arousal. The walk from the parking garage, the walk across the lobby of the Bellagio, the room check-in– all is of little importance to my lust-crazed mind.

I say a little prayer as we enter the elevator, hoping it's empty. Luck is on my side– empty. My calm dissolves the instant the elevator doors shut, trapping Rory in with me. I'm on him in a heartbeat, and he meets me halfway. A loud grunt is torn from our chests on impact.

"Beth, you drive me insane," Rory groans as he presses me up against the rear of the elevator. Our height difference is an inconvenience. Unable to reach Rory's lips without his help, I settle on feasting at his throat, biting him savagely. Rory's small sounds of protest amp up my hunger.

Large fingertips, roughened by callouses, skate up the backs of my thighs. Eager to feel Rory's body, I hook my calf around his ass, sandal digging into his tight buttocks. Finally putting me out of my misery, Rory bends down to connect our lips. A sigh escapes me at the sweet stroke, causing me to turn liquid. Rory's touch is slow, sure, reverent as he lovingly caresses my flesh. Lips slightly parted, our tongues tangle, weaving in and out of each other's mouths in a rhythmic dance.

"I can't wait any longer," I breathe, desperation and hunger twist my voice. "I need you to fill me... I need you inside me– finally."

"Bethany," Rory groans, fingers belying the protest in his voice. Hastily, Rory yanks up my dress, exposing my ass and cunny to the air. Bending at the knees, Rory roughly thrusts up against me, as if he's naked and impaling me. "Ugh!" we grunt together at the intense sensation of his bulge grinding into my naked pussy. Rory mounts me against the back wall of the elevator.

Fiercely kissing, hips grinding, lost to one another, we freeze at the whoosh of the elevator door opening. Rory instantly drops me to stand on shaky legs. I eye the door, hoping we're on our floor. Rory steps away from me until we are standing side-by-side with our luggage camouflaging the damp bulge in Rory's pants.

"What floor are we? This is twenty-two?" I ask out the side of my mouth as an elderly couple with a small dog slowly enters the elevator. Our exhibition would have curled their short hairs.

Sighing heavily, "Thirty-one. Let's hope it continues up before it takes our new companions to the lobby." Smiling angelically to lessen the impact of his mammoth size, "Hello, lovely morning, isn't it?"

Snickering underneath my breath, I try and fail to pull off angelic. The grandma is looking me over like I'm a cheap two-dollar-whore with my rumpled sundress, smelling like sex, lust-flushed cheeks and neck, kiss-swollen lips, and abraded face from Rory's beard. I roll my eyes to the ceiling and begin humming along with the Muzak.

"We just got married this morning," Chatty, TMI Rory announces happily. He takes my left hand, wraps it around the handle of the suitcase, proudly displaying my new wedding ring set. I look down at our joined hands with a silly grin tugging at my lips. I can't wait to stare at my left ring finger for hours... just as soon as I've had my fill of Mr. Essex, that is.

"Oh! Congratulations," Grandpa fawns all over us while Grandma is still eyeing me, trying to find my innermost guilt. The Yorkie is sniffing at my leg like it's its day job, and I say a silent prayer that the dog is too tiny to reach my thigh. I'm a dirty, sex-smelling girl right now.

Eyes returning to the ceiling, humming louder than ever, head now bobbing in time with the Muzak, I ask myself if this is the longest elevator ride in the history of elevator rides.

"Are you humming Aerosmith?" Rory asks me, sounding in disbelief. I give him a wide-toothed grin while nodding my head yes. "That's not what's playing. I think that's a Sinatra song." Rory has to bite his lip to stop himself from laughing convulsively.

The doors open, offering sweet salvation. I fly out, breathlessly gasping in relief over my newfound freedom. Now that we are blissfully alone, I begin singing instead of humming.

"I think we're just down the hall a bit. The lady at the front desk said our room was close to the middle of the hallway," Rory absentmindedly offers as he lugs our bags. "What are you singing?"

I belt out a bad rendition of the song, "*Love in an elevator. Lovin' it up when I'm goin' down. Love in an elevator. Lovin' it up when I hit the ground.*"

Rory doesn't laugh at me like I thought he would. Shoving the keycard into the door handle, he pulls off Steven Tyler better than Steven Tyler himself. "*Gonna be a penthouse pauper. Gonna be a millionaire. I'm gonna be a real fast talker... and have me a love affair. Gotta get my timin' right. It's a test that I gotta pass. I'll chase you all the way to the stairway, honey. Kiss your sassafras."*

Already weak-kneed and hotter than hell for my new husband, I'm near combustion levels as Rory's voice caresses my ears. Hearing those lyrics roll off his tongue all gravelly deep, like the perfect purr of a well-tuned *machine*, has me grabbing the man by the collar.

Rory releases a shocked gasp from my manhandling. I kick the luggage away as my palm smashes the door shut. "We were interrupted before…" my voice twists with seductive warning. Flipping the lock bar, "We won't be interrupted again."

Stepping backward, Rory tries to reason with me. Stammering, mouth dry, "Beth, it's our first time. Don't you want to go slow?"

"Remember our conversation on the plane?" I arch a brow in imitation of the person who would only go slowly with me. "Do you really want to take it slow?" I wait a heartbeat. "I know I don't. I'm sick of missionary in a bed. We can do that when we're old and gray." Stalking toward Rory, herding him back to whence we came, I trap him at the locked door. "I'm gonna ride you like a well-oiled machine purring underneath my drenched pussy."

Blue eyes bulging out of his skull, Rory got more than he bargained for with me. Face transforming from fright to awe, "I always knew you'd be a dirty talker." Rory turns the tables on me, using his immense size to push me up against the door. "Right now, I'm so out of my mind with need that I can't go slowly. I've waited an entire lifetime to have you, and I'm at the end of my patience."

"Good," a throaty purr rumbles up from my chest. My hands slide behind Rory's neck, gaining me the leverage I need to yank myself up. I wrap my legs around his hips, with my back pressing against the door. Confidence removes all of my worry and all of the usual fumbling. I reach down between us to unzip Rory's fly. "Fuck me. Hard. Fuck me like you're my husband, Mr. Essex."

Groaning, eyes closing in ecstasy at the sound of his name rolling off my tongue, "I'm always going to call you Mrs. Essex from now on, Bethany. Get used to it."

"AH!" is torn from my mouth when sharp teeth set into the delicate flesh of my neck. Rory bites me– hard. Head thumping back against the door, hand grasping at Rory's shoulder, my left hand yanks at anything in my way. Rory helps, but he's more concerned with shredding my wedding sundress, pulling it off my shoulder so he can continue his feast there.

"All I've thought about since you showed me your cock was having it thrusting deep inside me," I murmur in appreciation as my hand roughly yanks his fly open, hastily shoving his briefs out of the way with my fingertips. We both groan in unison as my hand grasps Rory's length, fingertips not meeting around its girth. A shudder works its way through Rory's body, and I luxuriate in the movement, loving how a simple touch can render the man stupid.

"Good God, you're huge," and I don't know if I'm speaking of Rory's massive body or his cock. I know Rory has always worried over his size, something that also plagues Auggie. But it only makes me feel more like a woman as Rory supports my entire weight with his palm grasping my bare ass. Not many women will have the pleasure of being able to scale their husband's body.

Gasping for breath, Rory pants near my ear as he continues to feast at my throat and shoulder: kissing, licking, nipping, and worshiping my skin. The sound alone causes beads of sweat to run down my spine. We're both hot in the arctic air-conditioned hotel room because we're both hot for each other.

My heels dig into Rory's hips, gaining leverage for me to open my thighs without falling to the floor. My fingernails bite into his shoulder as he presses me more firmly against the door. With a shaking hand, I press my husband's dick against my opening.

An intense shudder rolls through my body at the prospect of finally gaining what I've always longed to have. Rory– all mine. As a young girl, I knew I wanted something but I didn't know what. Now I realize I wanted it all: friendship, love, companionship, support, security, trust, and sex. I want all of Rory.

Angling my hips to take him in, Rory stops me with a squeeze to my buttocks. Voice thick, gruff, "I'll hurt you if you smash down on me. I don't look very long, but I'm thicker than you've ever had," he warns ominously, obviously knowing exactly how big the biggest I've ever had was.

Drawing in a deep breath, I use the courage, spontaneity, and freedom Rory infuses within me. I take Rory by surprise, his palm loosening enough to follow the movement of my ass.

Slamming my pussy down on Rory's cock, "You won't hurt me. It's going to feel incredible," comes out strangled from my throat when I take him inside.

I scream, and it's not from pain. A year of Auggie prepared me for my husband, and he never used all of his strength or length or prowess. I couldn't ever make that man lose control, because I wasn't supposed to. But here is a man I hold all the power over. Taking me at my word, Rory gives me all he's got, and then some.

"Christ!" Rory shouts as he impales me, cockhead butting my womb– it hurts so good. It's not gentle or loving. It's hunger, passion– involuntary. It's everything I need.

Fusing my body to Rory's, I grip him with my fingertips and toes, my arms and legs, and my pussy muscles. Panting wildly, sweat coating my skin, eyes rolling back in my head, I surrender to my husband. Instead of making our first time as husband and wife, our first time together ever, all about love and affection and commitment, Rory fucks me against the hotel room door… and it's glorious.

Rory's thrusts are more like lunges– strong thigh muscles bunching and releasing in a violent rhythm. He's so forceful my tits are spilling from my sundress to tap against my chin with every thrust. All I can do is hold on and grunt with every stroke.

"Your pussy is rubbing my dick raw," Rory gasps in exquisite pain. He bends down to capture my lips in a searing kiss, tongue darting in to take possession of my mouth. His calloused hands bruise my backside with the door brush-burning by back. Fully clothed with his cock jutting out of his pants, Rory's zipper is scratching a memento into my inner thigh. It's uncomfortable, but it makes me feel alive.

"Bed," Rory warns a split-second before the door is no longer supporting my back. I grab onto him for dear life, more scared of losing our connection than tumbling to the floor. Delirious, eyes half closed, Rory blindly carries me across the hotel room. His cock flexes inside me with every stride. A giggle is torn from my throat when we're almost up-ended by the luggage roadblock.

"Lil Pup, you're a naughty girl," Rory taunts as he roughly yanks me from his body, throwing me to the king-sized bed. Sprawled where Rory tossed me, I wait. "I'm gonna fuck you now," he warns, hands reaching to position me at the foot of the bed.

"What do you call what we were just doing, then?" I shriek when I'm maneuvered to my hands and knees, ass jutting off the edge of the bed. I shriek again, but this time it's from shocking pleasure. Bending down, Rory's tongue makes a pass against my swollen flesh. In one fast lick, he caressed me from my clit to my asshole. "AH!" I scream, shuddering, as Rory spits on my already drenched cunt.

"If you're rubbing me raw... Lord knows what I'm doing inside of you." Rory's voice is rough with satisfaction and awe. "I'm not complaining. I've never gone bareback, nor have I ever fucked someone before. I was always careful."

"Don't be careful," I beg. Ass waving like red at a charging bull, my eyes slip shut at the sensation of my nipples abrading against the fluffy white duvet.

"Remember that when you're hurting tomorrow... and the next day." Rory smacks my ass hard in example. Buttocks stinging, I grin against the duvet. A vanilla girl doesn't grow up to be a sex therapist, and Rory is just now realizing this.

"You liked that, did ya?" Laugher is lacing Rory's tone.

"Fuck!" I scream— impaled to my womb, stretched beyond measure, I'm going to be feeling that thrust for at least a week from now. Rory's fingertips snag my hair, strands twisting in his grip, and yank fiercely until my spine bows and my ass presses firmly against his pelvis.

Sensations warring between the savage violence and the tender affection, my eyelids flutter shut. Rory brushes soft open-mouthed kisses along my spine while he fucks me brutally. My skin tightens, dampens with sweat, rapidly cools, and then flashes with heat, as if it doesn't understand what's happening. My brain floods my system with a cocktail of intoxicating chemicals that roll my eyes back in my skull and have me writhing in ecstasy.

I continually grunt into the mattress. One sound of pain-filled protest melds into the song of pleasure, until I can no longer distinguish between the two. Rory's aggressive thrusts are so fast I can't discern where one ends and the next begins.

"Do you like me fucking you, Mrs. Essex?" Rory breathlessly demands. Shifting his hips, Rory gives me the hardest thrust yet, bruising my cunt with his cock and my ass with his hips. A scream is torn from my throat— half pain, half pleasure.

Blissed out, I lie on the mattress during Rory's onslaught. His hands are everywhere– yanking my hair, slapping my ass, squeezing my breasts, tugging and twisting my nipples. But it's what he does to my pussy that shoves me over the edge. Leaning over my back while violently thrusting, Rory's fingers are gentle, loving, as they caress my delicate flesh... and then Rory pinches my clit between his fingers and rolls it.

I shatter into a million pieces, screaming until no more sound is released from my throat. Mid-orgasm, with my body still shuddering from my release, Rory pulls from my body. He gently rolls me over, holding me in his arms. He slides us up the bed, and then settles between my thighs.

Rory makes love to me, as a husband to his wife, before I can even come down from my climax. Slowly rolling his hips against mine, tenderly stroking me from the inside with his cock, Rory treats me like his wife. He shows me how our first time would have been, if by some miracle we would have been born around the same time. Our age gap now is infinitesimal. But when we were a teen and a child, it was insurmountable.

I may not be a vanilla girl, but I'm not a rocky road chick, either. The fumbling sex with my classmates wasn't fulfilling, the monotonous sex with Auggie and Rob was boring, the one fucking from the pair was lacking, all because they weren't Rory. The intimacy, the affection, the connection was missing. Rory teaches me more in half an hour than all of my years of schooling and the year of education I had at Auggie's hands in the Playroom. The missing piece wasn't my sexuality, it was my husband. Whether he fucks me in an elevator, or makes love to me in a bed, it will always be special, electric, and amazing, because I'm in love with Rory. Always have been. Always will be.

Cupping my face in his palms, Rory stares down at me with eyes projecting all of his emotions: wonderment, satisfaction, trust, and love. The intensity strips me raw, bares my soul, and makes me feel like I have the world at my fingertips. I reach up and cup his face, stare into his eyes with all my emotions broadcasting across my features, and I make love to my husband as well.

Rory gives me everything. He gives me his all. He gives me the world... and I give it right back to him in return.

Tears glistening in my eyes, "I loved you before I even knew what the word meant. Thank you."

Smiling, doing his damnedest not to cry, Rory turns wry, "You're welcome."

Sighing, feeling content, happy, and at home for the first time in my life, I embrace my future. Cupping Rory's cheeks in my palms, my thumb brushes a tear away as it escapes the corner of his eye. "I love you, Mr. Essex."

Slowly lowering his face to mine for a kiss, Rory's words are a feather's brush against my flesh, "And I love you, Mrs. Essex... my Wildly Bedded Wife."

CHAPTER TWELVE

Stretching causes a loud groan to bubble up my throat. My God, I fucking hurt. I flex my muscles, trying to discern why they ache. I've been in two car accidents in my time, and they didn't hurt this badly. Those were fender-benders, and I feel as if I've been in a head-on collision with an eighteen-wheeler while in my sleep.

Wiggling around on the mattress, I try to find a comfortable spot. It's so dark in my room that I know I'm not due back at the salon for at least another few hours, meaning I should get up and put in a few hours on my thesis before I have to go in and stand on my feet for eight hours, washing hair and hating every second of it. I groan, dreading the endless small-talk with my patrons and the fallen arches of my soles.

I love people, but I love analyzing them more. What's difficult to swallow is the repetition of conversation: *the weather has been lovely/horrid/cold/hot/wet/dry. How is your daughter/son/brother/daughter/wife/husband? Yes, I'd love to hear about your medical aliments again.*

I was not cut out to cut hair for a living. I'm naturally chatty and completely weirded out by uncomfortable silence, so I've been dubbed a talker to fill the void while I style hair. I was born for one-on-one in a cozy office space, with all conversation centered on my patients' issues.

Stretching again, did I stay up too late writing on my thesis again? No, it's definitely more than a crick in the neck, and I'm not hugging my laptop like a pillow either.

"Ouch!" I yelp in pain when my thighs rub together. "Ow… ow… ow, that really freakin' hurts." Whimpering, I notice that the soreness is concentrated between my thighs. My puss feels beat up, bruised, ridden too hard, and rode again. I think back, memory foggy…

The one time Auggie screwed the hell out of me versus his usual kind routine, I wasn't this bad off. If the Beast couldn't harm me, what the hell did?

The further awake I become, the more noticeable the pain becomes. All the sore spots on my body are from being manhandled. Dimpled fingertip bruises, no doubt. Fiery pain shoots along my nerves when my nipples brush against the sheet covering me.

Room blanketed in darkness, I reach over to my side lamp. I need to check out my injuries before my imagination runs wild. My hand meets dead air. "What. The. Fuck?" I reach farther, still not finding my Hello Kitty lamp. Now that I'm awake, I realize the sheet covering me is not my Hello Kitty, fuzzy flannel sheet set, and the mattress beneath me is not twin-sized with springs jabbing into my ribcage.

Fear floods my veins as my mind rationalizes that I am NOT in my bedroom at home. My body has been ravaged, and I don't know how or by whom. As a woman on the cusp of a Master's in Psychology, working on her thesis, this scares the shit out of me.

Panting heavily into the dark room, my body tells me it's mid-morning, but the room itself is as dark as a coffin. My brain floods my body with a mixture of chemicals that set off a chain reaction: shaking, skin beading with gooseflesh, and sweat coating my skin as terror takes its hold.

"Little Pup," comes from a deep, husky voice. The sound of sheets shifting, as his body moves around on the bed, is loud to my hypersensitive ears.

The terror intensifies as I realize I am NOT the only occupant in this room, in this *bed*. Muscles bunching for flight, I take a deep breath, prepared to run even though I can't see.

"Bethany?" The tight voice is frustrated with me. "What is up with you, girl?"

A meaty palm reaches out to connect with my hand, squeezing as if to reassure me. I squeak, panicked. That huge hand put a beating on me. This man in bed with me has used and abused my body until it hurts so badly I can barely move. My heart starts to beat so rapidly I fear I'm going to have an attack– heart or panic, I'm not sure which.

Hand retracting, "Beth, goddamn it," he snarls as if disappointed in my rejecting his touch. Flesh slides on the sheets as he rolls to the edge of the bed. With him moving farther away from me, I take a deep breath and try to come up with an escape plan.

With an audible click, light floods the room, burning my eyes and causing me to blink repeatedly until my vision returns.

Haloed in the light, he's a large, fuzzy visage I can't quite make out.

"Are you blind?" he asks wryly as I blink up at him, amusement thick in his raspy voice. "Hung over, perhaps?" He chuckles to himself like he finds my terror entertaining, "Amnesiac?" I diagnose him as a sociopath right on the spot. Sounding way too pleased with himself, with a level of arrogance that pushes him into narcissism. Settling back against his pillow, he murmurs with utter satisfaction, "Give it a minute. It will all come flooding back in."

Between one blink to the next, he proves himself not arrogant but correct. "Motherfuck," I snarl, flailing around the bed in a fit of anger, not even giving a shit that it makes the pain between my thighs worse. "You tricked me, asshole!"

Blue eyes sparkling with mischief and pure pleasure, sinful lips displaying a Cheshire Cat smile, and one single dimple in his cheek, Rory crashes my world down around me. "Did you sleep well, Mrs. Essex?"

I arch my head back and laugh through the pain, confusion, and the tumultuous emotions. "Holy hell," I drawl out. "I woke up and thought I was back home in my tiny bed, as if it were several days ago." I stretch out my muscles while groaning in pain. "I fucking hurt," I blurt out.

Propped up on his elbow, Rory gazes down at me with a funny little smile twisting his lips. "You asked for it, and I always give my wife what she wishes."

I taunt Rory, because I'm a woman, and that's what we do. I sniffle, eyes watering, lips quivering.

"Oh, Christ, Bethany," Rory cries, sounding so sympathetic. He hovers over me, like he's scared to touch me. "I should have been gentler. I'm so sorry." A huge motherfucking grin splits my lips. "Lil Pup," Rory warns while shaking his head back and forth. "You're just asking for an ass beating."

Wearing a silly grin, "I'll deserve it. But give me a few days to recuperate first. My ass and puss are out of commission." I wince when my muscles contract, and it's not feigned.

"Did I hurt you that badly?" Rory looks appalled.

"You gave me exactly what I needed, exactly what I asked for, and will be asking for in about a week… or once a month." I reach up to tug Rory's lips down to mine. "Fuck me once a month, but make love to me every night, Mr. Essex."

Mouths fused together, Rory rolls over me, ready to do his husbandly duty. A sharp sound of protest spills from my lips into his mouth. "Ahh… maybe we better wait a few days, or at least until I take some pain relievers and have a soothing bath." Looking crestfallen, like he wants to beat himself up for being so rough, I assuage his guilt. "I loved it. I love you. Kiss me."

Rolling away from me, "Hey!" I shout at Rory when he abandons me on the bed. "Where are you going, mister?"

"My wife has requests." Rory stands by the side of the bed in all of his naked glory– almost six and a half feet of masculine perfection. Rory's body is gorgeous from generous genetics and hard work, and my children will be blessed to have him as their father. I close my eyes, saying a silent prayer of thanks to God.

Rory's all mine.

I'm all his.

"A kiss." My husband leans down to kiss my ring finger, smiling against my skin. Stalking away toward my handbag, Rory snatches it up and returns to my side. "Pain reliever." Pointing at the bathroom door, "A bath." Grabbing his cellphone, "Food."

Pleased beyond belief, I mutter, "What are you up to?"

"I'm proving my worth as a provider, and I will continue to do so until the day I die. Our crazy-with-happiness parents are moving your shit– minus any and all Hello Kitty paraphernalia– to our loft with Isis's supervision."

Cringing with embarrassment, "They're in for a rude awakening when they locate my sex treasure chest filled with my get-'er-off-ers."

"Isis," is all Rory says to comfort me on that front. Reaching into his suitcase, Rory retrieves something. Smiling sweetly, "And last but not least, a gift."

"OH! You got me something." I grab it out of Rory's hand, silently saying "oh, shiny." "You shouldn't have," I lie. I'm a girl, and we love presents. "I'll get you something when I'm no longer education rich-dirt poor."

"Having you is all I need." Rory's sincerity explodes my heart. Uncomfortable with the intense emotions, I tear into the oddly shaped present wrapped in paper decorated with gold wedding band sets.

"You think of everything," I marvel over the gift wrap. "R-O-R-Y!" I squeal. Forgetting all of the aches, pains, and bruises, I hop up to my knees in excitement. "You're the best husband a wife could ever dream." Unzipping the clear, plastic case, I grab the purple chalk while eyeing the glorious expanse of my husband's chest. "What do we decorate first?"

Pleased chuckles evolving into elated laughter, Rory is beyond proud of himself, and insanely happy. Grabbing a huge stick of pink chalk, "I thought we'd decorate your chest first… and then we can spend the rest of our days decorating Rush's huge parking lot with our kids and grandkids."

Never underestimating the power of fate. "And when it rains, we'll do it all over again."

Thank you for reading **WILDLY WEDDED WIFE**. Don't miss out on what's to come…
GOOD GIRL, Willow's coming-of-age tale.
WILDLY WEDDED WIFE, Rory & Bethany's novella.
WIDOW, Malcolm & Clover's journey.
WANTON, Opal & Ginny's tasty treat.
WARPED, Devon, Essie, Kieren, & Willow's future.
COMING SOON.
WOVEN, a novellas with surprising narrators.
WICKED, a novella showcasing Auggie & Tina's parents.
WAYWARD, Auggie, Isis, and Robin's angsty emotional roller coaster ride.
…and many more to come

ACKNOWLEDGEMENTS

A lot of work goes into writing a novel, and it isn't just by the writer herself. **My parents:** for their unconditional support. **My readers**: thank you for reading my twisted words and spreading my books to the masses. For without you, no one would've ever heard of my stories. My readers are my lifeblood. A shout out to the members of the **M&M of Restraint Group on Facebook**: thanks for the endless entertainment and inspiration. **Wicked Reads**: (in all its incarnations) **Angela G.**, thank you for taking over and making Wicked Reads better than I could have done by myself. & thank you for helping promote my work and the work of other authors. Angela? Have I told you lately how much I appreciate you? A huge thank you to the **Wicked Writer's Betas** for keeping me grounded and encouraging me to keep trudging along when I get frustrated. Your thoughts and observations are invaluable. ((Hugs)) Beta readers: **Kris | Suz | Darcy | Sandy | Di | Angela | Diane | Jacki | Linsey | Alexis | Billie Jo | Tassie | Caroline | Judith | Jodi Lynn | Jodi |** Someday, I'd love to meet you all in real life– it would be the experience of a lifetime.

ABOUT THE AUTHOR

Erica Chilson does not write in the 3rd person, wanting her readers to *be* her characters. Therefore, writing a bio about herself, is uncomfortable in the extreme.

Born, raised, and here to stay, the Wicked Writer is a stump-jumper, a ridge-runner. Hailing from North Central Pennsylvania, directly on the New York State border; she loves the changes in seasons, the humid air, all the mountainous forest, and the gloomy atmosphere.

Introverted, but not socially awkward, Erica prides herself on thinking first and filtering her speech. There are days she doesn't speak at all. If it wasn't for the fact that she lives with her parents, giving her a sense of reality, she would be a hermit, where the delivery man finds her months after expiration.

Reading was an escape, a way to leave a not-so pleasant reality behind. Reading lent Erica the courage she gathered from the characters between the pages to long for a different life. Writing was an instrument of change, evolving Erica into the woman she is today– a better, more mature, more at peace thinker.

Erica has a wicked mind, one she pours out into her creations. Her filter doesn't allow all of it to erupt, much to her relief. Sarcastic, with a very dark, perverse sense of humor, Erica puts a bit of herself into every character she writes.

I love hearing from readers. If you would like more information on release dates, works in progress, teaser chapters, and random bits of madness, please visit my Facebook Fan Page: https://www.facebook.com/thewickedwriter my website: ericachilson.com or please contact me via email: wickedwriter.ericachilson@gmail.com
DEVIANTS ONLY, if you'd like to join Erica Chilson's closed Facebook group, M&M of Restraint: https://www.facebook.com/groups/MistressandMaster/

www.ingramcontent.com/pod-product-compliance
Lightning Source LLC
Chambersburg PA
CBHW070505130626
46555CB00003B/1169